U0142288

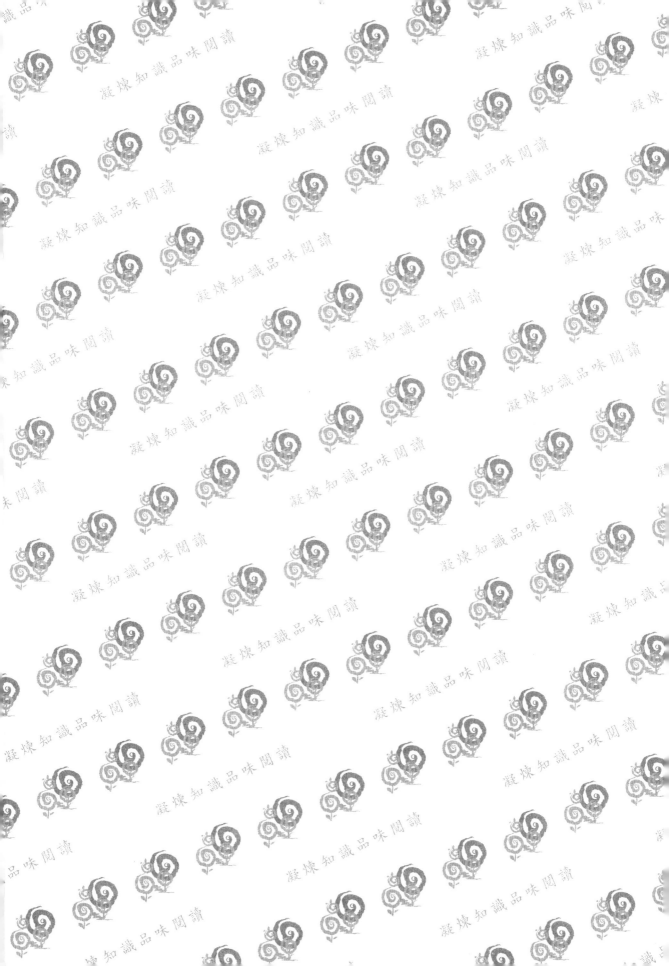

IMO
General Maritime English Conservations

初級

航海英語會話

王鳳敏 —— 著

航海
海上氣象
描述工作
岸上
通訊

海上氣象
情境會話 點餐
航海字彙 自我介紹
通訊 描述工作
訂房 岸上問路
生活日常

五南圖書出版公司 印行

自序
編輯說明

　　全球貨物運輸大多藉由海運輸送，我國船隊載運能量已佔全球重要地位。近年來遠洋客輪和私人遊艇亦蓬勃發展，使得航海人員需求數量增長快速，航海人員的素質也倍受關注，特別是英語能力，關係著海上人命、財產與船舶安全，海洋環境保護，及提升團隊高效能營運。由於許多海難事件是因海事英語使用不當造成，聯合國海事組織（IMO）在 1995 年修訂「船員訓練、合格和當值航行標準」（Standards of Training , Certification and Watchkeeping）公約，明訂英語為海事工業的官方語言，並發展出海事英語之典範課程綱要〔Model Course 3.17〕，說明船員所需具備的英語能力指標和知識內涵。該課綱還建議，各國實施海事英語教學時，須考量學習者對一般英語及海事專業知識的掌握程度，自行刪除或調整這些能力指標，或另選擇一些教材料來彌補學習者現有的知識能力和典範課程目標之間的差距。然而各國船員訓練機構大都只提供航海機械操作和技能訓練，海事英語書籍也都以航海知識內容和技能為範疇，且非由語言教師授課，非英語為母語的學生在英語語言的部分得自學；歐盟 1999 年的多元文化和多語船員對運輸影響之年度報告，建議各國海事學校必須先建立適合自己學生的初級英語能力標準，學生達成此標準後再進入所謂的海事英語訓練階段。

　　亞洲地區是非英語為母語國際船員的主要供應來源，然而卻無以語言學習觀點和航海學習者實際使用英語的情境，出版的航海生活英語會話教材。市面的一般英語會話教材雖多，內容包羅萬象，航海人員不易於短時間內找到直接相關航海生活情境的會話教材。基於以上因素，本書為輔助我國將進入海事訓練或相關工作，或對航海英語會話有興趣的人員編寫，以 2015 年聯合國海事組織出版的 Model Course 3.17 中的 General Maritime English（GME）所規範的基礎級（Elementary Level） 18 項能力指標為架構和目標，編寫了航海環境中的生活和工作情境內容，包括自我介紹、描述工作、岸上餐廳點餐、訂房、問路、通訊、海上氣象等，強調航海生活中使用英語溝通表達的人際互動，並提供航海英文的基本字彙、常用英語文法及語用功能。有別於航海課程的專業內容，操船舵令之類的技術與用語非本書重點。期以航海生活的英語會話為目標，幫助學習者順利養成良好的英語溝通能力，進而享受航海生涯。

本書撰寫歷經以下 3 個階段：

1. 參照 IMO Model Course 3.17 的 GME 基礎級英語能力指標，並訪談我國資深船長關於船員工作與生活中實際使用英語的需求。

2. 考量我國一般海事相關科系學生之英語程度，研擬各單元教學目標、內容撰寫、編排方式。

3. 蒐集國內外資料撰寫課文內容。由於實際航海生活中，偏重英語聽說技能，航海人員接觸非英語為母語的人士機會非常多，需適應不同地方腔調的英語口音，本書課文大部分有錄音，且提供不同地方的英語口音為範例，和許多練習題，讓學習者能反覆練習，成為本書特色。

課文含十個主題單元，每單元分四部分，第一部分為兩篇主要對話範例、發音、聽說練習；第二部分為常用的航海英語文法、語用功能和文化意涵等說明及練習；第三部分為背景知識的短文閱讀和練習；第四部分延伸更多聽說寫的練習題。藉活潑生動的人物對話、海事故事、練習題和聽力，提供大量語言練習的機會，來增進學習者的聽說理解和表達能力。所有內容經國內兩位航海專家教授和三位外籍英語教師審稿校正。由英語為母語人士在專業錄音室中錄製成 MP3。除課本和 MP3 外，還有「學習手冊」，提供每課對應 Model Course 3.17 的能力指標爲何，學習內容的中文解說和延伸的學習材料指引。

　　本書編寫過程接受國內許多關心海事英語的機構人士和學者所提供的資源和支持鼓勵才得以出版，銘記在心，但無法於此全部致謝。誠摯地將出版成果特別歸功於長榮海運公司公關部惠予照片和長榮海事博物館田本源館長諮詢，國立海洋大學李國添前校長、張清風前校長支助並鼓勵出版，李選士前副校長提供最新 Model Course 3.17 2015 Edition，商船學系林彬教授和翁順泰教授義務審稿，輪機工程學系華健教授、應用英語研究所鍾正倫老師提供諮詢，空中美語外籍師資團隊校稿和錄音，和張珮儀老師創作插畫。

CONTENTS

目　錄

單元 Unit Topic	主題 Theme	目標 Lesson Objectives	相關的英語能力指標 IMO Model Course Indicators
1. Welcome aboard!	Meeting new people on board	Greeting; introducing a friend to another; talking about self; nationality and people; describing location	1. Ask for and give personal data
2. Who else works on the ship?	Describing crew, work routines, and life at sea	Describing crew roles and responsibilities; describing physical appearance and personality; saying time at sea; describing leisure time on board	2. Describe crew roles and routines; 7. Describe working as a team on board 11b. Passenger information 13a. Describe visitors on board
3. I like fresh food better.	Talking about food on board	Describing preferences regarding food; naming items of food and drink; describing quantities, weights; ordering food	7. Express personal likes and dislikes 9. Express personal preferences; discuss food on board 11. Check supplies, quantities, weights
4. What kind of vessel is it?	Vessel information	Name types of vessels; compare vessel details; the International Code of Signals; booking hotels	3. Name types of vessels 12. Compare vessel details
5. Where's the Master's cabin?	Places and equipment on board	Describing vessel parts and equipment; naming positions and describing locations; asking for and giving directions on board and ashore	6. Name positions on board; give directions on board and ashore
6. What is the safety equipment for?	Safety equipment and internal communications in emergency situations on board	Describing various devices of safety equipment for emergencies and their functions including personal protective equipment; understanding instructions, internal communications and commands in emergency situations on board	4. Identify the location and purpose of safety equipment 10. Understand commands in emergency situations on board

單元 Unit Topic	主題 Theme	目標 Lesson Objectives	相關的英語能力指標 IMO Model Course Indicators
7. Is it safe at sea?	Marine casualties	naming marine incidents and reports; distress calls; SMCP for urgency communication	10. Understand commands in emergency situations on board 15a. Report events from the past 16. Report details of incidents at sea 18b. VHF communications for distress and urgency messages
8. I request urgent medical advice.	Medical emergencies	Understanding physical injuries at sea; describing illness and symptoms; naming First Aid items and functions; making a request for medical assistance	17. Request medical assistance 12b. Deal with health and safety on board
9. How's the weather?	Weather forecast	Understanding BBC shipping forecast; understanding inshore waters forecast; understanding weather report on land	14. Describe weather conditions; understand forecasts
10. Do not overtake the vessel ahead of you.	Departure and arrival	Using latitude and longitude to describe geographic locations; understanding standard helm orders; producing VHF external spoken communications to request and give advice with VTS; checking task completion in routine operations on leaving a port	5. Discuss navigational routes and geographic locations; understand standard helm orders 8a. Describe routine operations on board 18a. Check task completion in routine operations

Unit 1 Welcome aboard!

Part One: Meeting New People

Conversation 1 : It's nice to meet you.

Scenario: The Lucky Venture, a cargo ship, moors in the harbor. Jack boards the ship with his friend Keiko. His uncle, Captain Johnson greets them.

gangway

Pre-listening Questions:
1. Who is the girl?
2. Where is she from?

2

Conversation 1 : 🎧 Track 1

Jack:	Hi, Uncle Paul.
Captain Johnson:	Good to see you, Jack.
Jack:	I'd like you to meet my friend, Keiko Kato.
	She's an exchange student.
Captain Johnson:	It's nice to meet you, Miss Kato. Welcome aboard.
Keiko:	Thank you. It's a pleasure to meet you, sir.
Jack:	My uncle has spent much of his life at sea. He's an experienced captain.
Captain Johnson:	Well, I enjoy the sea very much. What part of Japan are you from?
Keiko:	I was born and raised in Kobe, but my parents are originally from Hokkaido.
Jack:	Hokkaido? Is it far from Kobe?
Keiko:	Yes. Kobe is located in the southwest on Honshu Island, the main island of Japan. And Honshu Island is south of Hokkaido.
Captain Johnson:	Hokkaido is situated in the northern part of the Japanese archipelago at about the same latitude as Chicago, Montreal and Rome. Kobe is a beautiful international port city. I've been there many times. I like the city very much. By the way, our Chief Officer is waiting for you. He'll show you around. Let me introduce you to him.

Comprehension Questions : 🎧 Track 2

1. What did Jack say to introduce Keiko to his uncle?
2. What is Keiko's last name?
3. What is Captain Johnson's first name?
4. What other information did Jack give besides the names when he made introductions?
5. Where is Hokkaido?

Conversation 2 : Where are you from, sir? 🎧 Track 3

Scenario: The Chief Officer is meeting Jack and Keiko.

Chief Officer:	It's a pleasure to meet you. I'm the Chief Officer. I believe you want to see some places on the ship. Are you two students?
Jack & Keiko:	Yes, we are.
Jack:	I'm studying in the Department of Merchant Marine. I'm going to sail with a ship to Greece for the one-year sea-going practice this summer.
Chief Officer:	Great! You'll serve as the navigating cadet. Are you excited about it?
Jack:	Definitely. That's why I can't wait to tell my uncle about it.
Chief Officer:	How about you? Excuse me. What's your name again?
Keiko:	Keiko. I won't be able to be a cadet on board because I'm majoring in English Literature. I'm Japanese. Where do you come from, sir?
Chief Officer:	Please call me Carlos. I'm from Colombia.
Keiko:	A country in South America?
Chief Officer:	Right. My country is very beautiful. It borders the Caribbean Sea, between Panama and Venezuela.
Keiko:	I'd like to visit your country some day.
Chief Officer:	You will love Colombia!

Comprehension Questions : 🎧 Track 4

1. What is Jack major?
2. What is Jack going to do this summer?
3. Why can't Keiko serve as a navigating cadet?
4. Where is the Chief Officer from?
5. Where is Colombia?

Pronunciation: Word Stress 🎧 Track 5

● ·	· ●	· ● · ·	· · ●	· · ● · ·
welcome	exchange	experienced	introduce	Venezuela
pleasure	enjoy	Colombia		
captain	aboard			
northern	Japan			

Part Two: Grammar, Cultural and Language Tips

A. Common phrases to ask about nationality and to give the answer

1.Where	are you / they	from?
	is he / she	

I'm		Korea.
He / She is	from	Japan.
They are		Thailand.

2.Where	do you / they come	from?
	does he / she come	

I	come from	Korea.
They		Japan.
He / She	comes from	Thailand.

3. What's	your / her / his nationality?

My / Her / His nationality	is	American.
I	am	Chinese

* Fill in the blanks based on the table information.

1. Li-Li Wang is from _____ . She is _____ .
2. Where is Masao from? He is from _____ He is _____ .
3. What is Oscar's family name? His family name is _____ .
4. Is Oscar from Chile? _____ .
5. Is Marco Mexican? _____ .
6. Where does Carlos come from? _____ .
7. Where _____ Keiko and Masao from? They _____ from Japan.

Person's Name Family Name / Surname, First Name / Given Name	Country Name	Adjective of Nationality
Wang, Li-Li	Taiwan	Taiwanese
Tanaka, Masao	Japan	Japanese
Agus	Indonesia	Indonesian
Garcia, Oscar	Chile	Chilean
Martinez, Marco	Mexico	Mexican
Perez, Carlos	Colombia	Colombian
Rivera, Roberto	Puerto Rico	Puerto Rican
Poggi, Gina	Italy	Italian

* Find the following nations on a world map through the Internet, and write down people from the nations.

Taiwan	
Japan	

Malta	
Vietnam	

Cuba	
Colombia	
Indonesia	
Australia	
Romania	
Malaysia	
Singapore	
Chile	
Brazil	
Panama	
Canada	
Puerto Rico	
Mexico	
Bahamas	
Egypt	

Pakistan	
Somalia	
New Zealand	
Finland	
Denmark	
Norway	
Turkey	
France	
Philippines	

B. Describing Locations of Countries and Cities

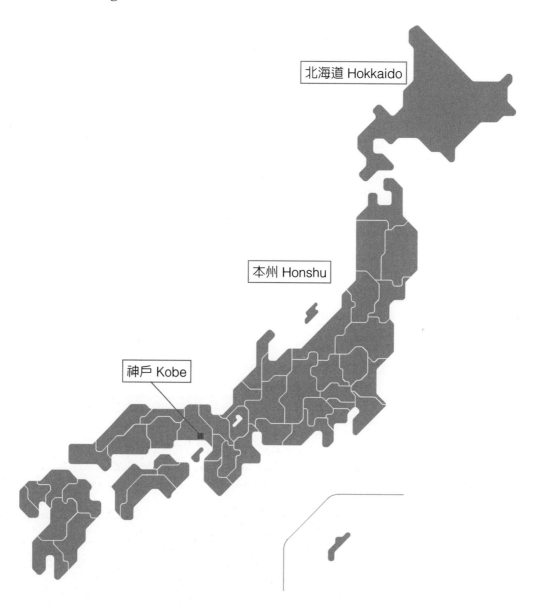

北海道 Hokkaido

本州 Honshu

神戸 Kobe

Kobe is a harbor city in Japan. It is located on the southern side of Honshu. Honshu is the largest and most populous island of Japan. Honshu is located south of Hokkaido. The island of Hokkaido is located in the north of Japan. The following sentences are the ways people used to express precise meanings of a particular place. Pay attention to the different prepositions.

Describing a location in a larger area:

Kobe is located **in** Japan.

101 Building is located **in** Taipei.

Greece is located i**n the southeastern region of** the European Continent.

Colombia is located **in the northeastern part of** South America, bordering the Caribbean Sea, between Panama and Venezuela.

Italy is **in the south of** Europe.

Keelung **is in northern Taiwan**.

Kenting **is in southern Taiwan**.

Describing a location in a smaller place or a specific address:

The Maritime Museum is located **at/within** my school.

Singapore is situated **at the southernmost tip of** the Peninsular Malaysia.

The factory is located **at** 3rd Floor, No.435 Madison St., New York.

Others:

My school is located **near/by** the river.

He is located i**n this building**, but I do not know which floor.

The factory is located **on this street**.

The Grand Canyon is located **on the North American continent**.

Spain's third biggest airport is located almost 70 km **to the southwest of** Port de Pollenca.

Taiwan **lies between** the Philippines **and** Japan.

Taiwan **is(lies) to the south of** Japan.

C. Review Subject Pronouns and Object Pronouns

Identify the positions of nouns, subject pronouns and object pronouns in the sentences.

Nouns	Subject pronouns	Object pronouns
My name is Keiko Kato.	I'm Japanese.	Please call me Keiko.
Jack's uncle enjoys sea very much.	He is an experienced captain.	Jack and Keiko are visiting him.
Keiko is Japanese.	She is an exchange student.	Jack is standing beside her.
Jack and Keiko go to the same school.	They boarded the ship together.	The Chief Officer will show them around.

Practice: Your turn to complete the sentences

1. A: I need the compass. Please give it to _____ .   B: Here you are.

2. A: Where is the Captain?   B: I don't know. _____ is not here.

3. A: When should I come to meet him?

   B: I don't know. Why not call _____ to find out.

4. A: Who are _____?   B: Jack and Keiko.

D. Word Study

1. **aboard** *adv. or prep.*

   ☞ Go aboard.

   ☞ All aboard!

2. **abroad** *adv.*

   ☞ He went abroad for study.

   ☞ He is from abroad.

   ☞ He was sent abroad.

3. **board** *v. or n.*

   ☞ to board a ship (to get on a ship, to embark a ship)

   ☞ on board

4. **boarding pass** *n.*

May I have your boarding pass?

5. **overboard** *adv.* (over the side of a ship into the water)

man overboard

6. **broad** *adj.*

☞ The box is three feet broad.

☞ She has broad views.

7. **broadcast** *v. n. or adj.*

The BBC broadcasted the news this morning.

He gave the broadcast.

Did you watch the broadcast news yet?

Part Three: Reading

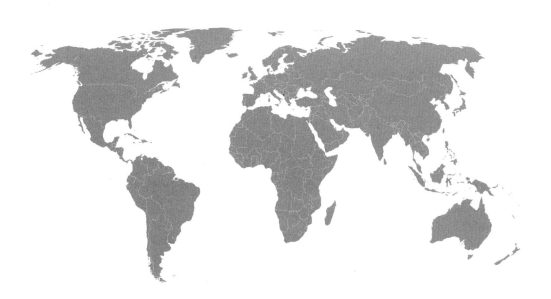

Shipping was the world's first global industry. It has grown rapidly in recent years with dramatic increases in size and passenger capacity. The cargo shipping industry is continuously expanding because more than 80 percent of the volume of world trade is transported by sea. Owing to the impact of the Covid-19 pandemic and resulting travel restrictions, delays deliveries even threaten to drive up costs of shipping for an unprecedented supply chain impact.

The crew on board comes from different countries over the world. The majority of the shipping industry's seafarers are from nations where English is not the native language. About two thirds of the world's merchant marine is manned by a crew composed of several nationalities in one ship at the same time. In 1995, the IMO designated English as the official language for seafarers taking into consideration that the ability to properly convey information is important not only to the safety of shipping but also to the well being of crew. Crew mixture can bring about problems in interaction due to cultural and communication differences. It is essential for seafarers to have the art of effective communication and use correct English language in the maritime environment.

Comprehension Questions :

1.) What does the author say about shipping?

    a) Shipping was the world's first global industry but it is not that important any more.

    b) The development of cargo shipping industry is destroyed by the impact of the Covid-19 pandemic and resulting travel restrictions.

    c) The world relies on cargo shipping industry a lot.

2.) Which is not the reason for the IMO to designate English as the official language for seafarers?

    a) For the majority of seafarers, English is not their native language.

    b) Proper communication is important both for the safety of shipping and the crew.

    c) English people are the majority in the maritime industries.

3.) According to the passage, what can affect the safety of the ship?

    a) Cultural and communication differences.

    b) Too many crew members on a ship.

    c) Large size and passenger capacity..

Part Four: More Exercises

A. Say and Write in English

1. 船長是臺灣來的。他是臺灣人。

_____

2. 歡迎上船！

_____

3. 很高興認識你。

_____

4. 我在哥倫比亞出生和成長。

_____

5. 他是個很有經驗的船員。

_____

6. 新加坡位於馬來半島最南端。

_____

7. 本州島在北海道南方。

_____

8. 我主修商船。

_____

9. 我是大二學生。

_____

B. Listen and Answer : 🎧 Track 6

1.) What is the man's nationality?

    a) American   b) Indonesian   c) Puerto Rican   d) Indian

2.) What does the man do?

    a) A cook   b) A seafarer   c) A mechanic   d) A bowler

3.) Which of the following activity would the man do when not working on board?

    a) Dining out with friends

    b) Dining at home with friends

    c) Playing golf with friends

    d) Go sailing with friends

4.) What does the man plan to do in the future?

    a) Change his job.   b) Marry a girl.

    c) Go to school again.   d) Be a mechanic.

C. Check out the location of the following cities through the Internet.

    1. Shanghai

    _____

    2. Copenhagen

    _____

D. Fill in the "Getting to Know You" Preparation Worksheet and share the information with your classmate.

Getting to Know You

1. What's your name?

   _____

2. Does your name have a special meaning?

   _____

3. Where are you from?

   _____

4. Where were you born? Where were you raised?

   _____

5. What is your hometown like?

   _____

6. What is your major?

   _____

7. Which high school did you go to?

   _____

8. How do you like your high school life?

   _____

9. Are you working now full-time? Part-time?

   _____

10. Are you married or single? Engaged?

   _____

11. Who do you live with now?

   _____

12. hat do you think would be an ideal job or career for you in the future?

   _____

13. What do you enjoy doing in your free time?

   _____

14. What hobbies or special interests do you have?

   _____

<table>
<tr><td>Unit
2</td><td># Who else works on
the ship?</td></tr>
</table>

Part One: What do you do on board?

Conversation 1 : Deck officers and their key responsibilities

Scenario: The Chief Officer is explaining the shipboard personnel and their responsibilities to Keiko.

Bridge, picture from EVERGREEN.com

Pre-listening Questions:

1. Who is the head of the Deck Department?
2. Where are they going after the conversation?

Conversation 1 : 🎧 Track 7

Keiko: What do you do on board?

Chief Officer: Generally speaking, I assist the Captain in the general administration. I'm also responsible for cargo operation, navigation, and ship maintenance.

Keiko: That's a lot of work. Is there anyone who can help you?

Chief Officer: Yes, several people in fact: the Second Officer, the Third Officer... You see, the tall guy with brown hair, who's checking the navigation equipment over there. He's the Second officer, a very good helper to me but he doesn't talk much. He's in charge of all navigation equipment and charts.

Keiko: I see. Who's the one with moustache, standing by the wheel?

Chief Officer: The Helmsman. He's the person who actually steers the vessel, a gentle guy from Scotland. The Third officer is not here. You might see him later, a big guy with gray hair and very funny man. He talks a lot, and play jokes on others. We also have Bosun, Petty officers and deckhands in the deck department.

Keiko: You have very nice people working here, right?

Chief Officer: Right. I'm lucky to have them.

Keiko: Is Captain Johnson the head of the deck department?

Chief Officer: I am, but all crew on board are under the Captain's command. He supervises all the departments.

Keiko: How many departments do you have?

Chief Officer: We have deck, engine and catering departments.

Keiko: Can I visit the engine department?

Chief Officer: Sure. Please follow me down these stairs one level. The engine room is below this deck. I'd like to introduce you to some of the crew who works in the engine department.

Comprehension Questions : 🎧 Track 8

1. What does the Chief Officer do?
2. Who is in charge of all navigation equipment and charts?
3. Who actually steers the vessel?
4. What does the Third Office look like?
5. How many departments are on this ship?

Conversation 2 : Third Engineer's Duties 🎧 Track 9

Scenario: Keiko is chatting with the Fourth Engineer about his work in the engine room.

Engine room, picture from EVERGREEN.com

Keiko:　　　　　　　When do you keep the Engine room watch?

Fourth Engineer:　I stand watch from 08:00 to 12:00 and 20:00 to 24:00.

Keiko:　　　　　　　What do you do during the watch?

Fourth Engineer:　Well, I inspect the engine room, the steering gear room, the emergency fire pump compartment and the air conditioning compartment. I check the correct functioning of all automatic control, electrical and monitoring systems, and see if there's enough oil or water inside them.

Keiko:　　　　　　　You must keep some spare parts for repairs, right?

Fourth Engineer: Yes, I'm also in charge of the inventory of spare parts.

Keiko: How about the fire fighting equipment here? Do you need to test them very often?

Fourth Engineer: Sure. I carry out the test at least once per month for them to ensure they are always in top condition.

Keiko: What would you do if you found a serious problem with a machine or equipment?

Fourth Engineer: I would immediately notify the Chief Engineer, wait for his order, and. put it in the Engine Logbook

Keiko: How do you like your job?

Fourth Engineer: Very much. I have the patience to dismantle machines and figure out why it isn't working. I like that. Besides, the working environment here is good. We have modern machines and facilities. In my leisure time, I play table tennis with other seafarers or go to the fitness center.

Keiko: Sounds great!

Comprehension Questions : 🎧 Track 10

1. When does the Fourth Engineer perform his duty watch?
2. What does he do during the watch?
3. How often does the Fourth Engineer carry out the test for the fire fighting equipment?
4. Why does the Fourth Engineer carry out the test?
5. Who should the Fourth Engineer report to when he finds serious problem in the engine room?

Pronunciation: Word Stress 🎧 Track 11

• ·	· •	• · ·
duty	assist	operate
fighting	indeed	monitor
normal	ensure	notify
engine	report	

· • ·	• · · ·	· • · ·
maintenance	regularly	responsible
condition		immediate
equipment		
abnormal		

· · •	· · • ·
engineer	navigation

Part Two: Grammar, Language, and Cultural Tips

A. The Organization of Ship Crew

The formal title for the man in charge of a ship is Master, though he is often addressed as "Captain". He must be an experienced navigator and properly qualified for command.

The organization of the crew of a ship is varied. It depends on the ship's company and the ship's size. It is customary to find Deck and Engine Departments on board. Each department is made up of a varied number of officers（甲級船員）and ratings（乙級船員）.

The head of the Deck Department is the Chief Officer, often called as First Mate. He could be assisted by a First Officer/Mate, a Second Officer/Mate, a Third Officer/Mate, and sometimes a Fourth Officer/Mate. Boatswain/Bosun（水手長）directs a number of ratings like AB（Able Seamen 幹練水手）, OS（Ordinary Seamen 水手）, Efficient Deck Hands（高效甲板手）, and other grades of seamen.

The Chief Engineer is responsible for the Engine Department. He is assisted by a Second, Third, Fourth and sometimes Fifth Engineer or an Electrical Officer. The engine room ratings may include Motor Man（機匠）, Oiler（油匠）.

On cruse ships, you will find the Department of Catering, which prepares excellent food for all people on board. On a cargo ship, there are a Chief Cook and some Mess Boys.

B. Examples of Common Personal and Duties

Position	Department	Responsibility
Captain/Master		is in charge of safety and welfare of ship, its cargo, crew and passengers.
Chief Officer/ Chief Mate	Deck	oversees deck department, ship maintenance, cargo operation, and navigation
Second Officer/ Second Mate	Deck	is responsible for navigation instrument, charts and navigation
Third Officer/ Third Mate	Deck	is responsible for maintenance of the life-saving equipment, fire-fighting installations and navigation
Helmsman	Deck	steers the ship
Bosun	Deck	manages deck ratings
Chief Engineer	Engine room	oversees engine operation maintenance, and personnel
Second Engineer	Engine room	checks the correct functioning of all automatic control, electrical and monitoring system
Third Engineer	Engine room	maintains electrical supply and equipment
Fourth Engineer	Engine room	does the fuel, oil, oil tanks and deck machinery maintenance
Chief Cook	Catering	prepares meals, controls his galley crew

✱ Useful expressions:

He is responsible for + Noun (things)   He checks + Noun (things)

He is in charge of + Noun (things)   He prepares + Noun (things)

He maintains + Noun (things)   He supervises + Noun (person)

He oversees+ Noun (things)   He controls + Noun (things)

He directs + Noun (things)

Examples: The chief mate is responsible for the vessel's cargo operations, its stability, and supervising the deck crew. The chief mate typically stands the 4-8 navigation watch and directs the bridge team.

Bosun instructs ratings to perform some tasks on the deck.

The trainer encouraged them to maintain their recent improvement.

✱ Directing cleaning actions:

Scour/scrub off the dirt/oil from the floor.

Scrub the sinks with cleanser.

Sweep the floor.

Wax the floor

Wipe the dishes.

Wipe off the window

Vacuum the carpet.

C. Shipboard Routine

Ships follow standard routine for operation in port and at sea. For example, a Plan of the Day will be issued to give information of the ship's routine. The Officer of the Deck (OOD) will distribute the plan to all offices and direct the crew to work out the plan. Watch-standing duties are the major ones in the plan. The watch-standing duties are carried out on a 24-hour a day basis at sea. Each watch-standing is usually four hours duration. If watch standers have failed to perform their job, the mistakes may cause a collision, grounding, and even the loss of a ship.

In port, Officer of the Deck is responsible for the Safety of the ship and carries out the plan of the day for port watches. The followings are examples of shipboard watches:

Anchor Watch – task as veering chain or adjusting lines to assist the OOD during the night

Main Engine and Auxiliary Watches – maintaining the operational readiness of main and auxiliary engines

Bridge & Signal Watch – keeping the OOD informed on notable changes in weather, boats approaching the ship and unusual disturbances or distress in harbor

Cold Iron Watch – inspecting secured machinery spaces

Electrical Equipment Watch – the maintenance of electrical equipment

Quarter Master of the Watch – assisting the OOD in navigation and reporting all changes in weather, temperature and making appropriate entry in the QM logbook

Radioman of the Watch – maintaining required communication in the radio room

Deck Petty Officer of the Watch (Deck POW) and messenger– assisting the OOD

Oil King – recording fuel soundings

D. Saying Time at Sea 🎧 Track 12

Time should be expressed in the 24 hour notation at sea.

On land:	At sea:
four o'clock in the morning	⟶ 0400
four o'clock in the afternoon	⟶ 1600

It's your turn. Say the time at sea.

1. nine o'clock in the morning ⟶
2. nine o'clock in the evening ⟶
3. eleven fifteen in the morning ⟶
4. eleven fifteen in the evening ⟶

E. Describing Ship Crew or Passengers

He is tall and thin.

He's got spiked hair.

He has thick eyebrows.

He is easy going.

He's bald.

He has a beard and a mustache.

He is plump.

He has a really nice smile.

She has round face.

She has curly black hair.

She wears glasses.

She is in her late sixties.

She has a good temper.

She has oval face.

She's got straight blond hair.

She wears her hair in a ponytail.

She is slim.

She is shy and conservative.

He's very muscular.

He's about average height.

He is good-looking.

He is polite and responsible.

F. Question Intonations 🎧 Track 13

Questions end with a rising pitch.

1. Does the Master keep a watch?

2. Are you students?

3. Can I visit the engine department?

4. Would you like to sit down?

5. Do you need to test them too?

6. Did you report it yet?

7. You must store spare parts for fixing, right? (expecting that the answer is positive)

Questions end with a falling pitch.

1. When do you keep the Engine room watch?

2. How about fire fighting equipment here?

3. What do you do during the watch?

4. Who's the one with moustache, standing by the wheel?

5. What would you like, tea or Coffee?

G. Prepositions for phrases relating to time

The Captain was awoken **at midnight**.

The crewmember had their lunch **at noon**.

The Chief Office was born **in 1960**.

The Chief Engineer's birthday is **in July**.

The test of main engine will be **in May, 2013**.

The weather is not cool here **in fall**.

The Titanic left England **on April 10, 1912**.

The ship will sail from New York **on February 23rd**.

The ship will discharge gas oil on **Tuesday**.

The maintenance should be finished **by the appointed time**.

The fire-fighting installation must be done **by tomorrow**.

The Second Engineer checked the correct functioning of all automatic control **till late afternoon**.

First Watch is **from 2000 to midnight**.

The Captain was on the bridge **during the time** the ship is entering the harbor.

H. Simple Present, Simple Past, and Simple Future

Simple Present: (a) indicating a situation/event that exists at present or habitually, for example describing an activity/routine work;

Examples: The pilot is on board at present.

I record and report abnormal conditions of the main engine.

(b) indicating something that was true in the past, is true in the present, and will be true in the future

Examples: I'm from Taiwan. / I'm Taiwanese. Taiwan. / I'm xxx

My parents live in Korea.

＊ When in Third Person Singular:

Verb be

The Chief Officer is the head of the deck department.

The Second Officer **checks** all navigation equipment and charts.

Other verbs

He **goes** to the fitness center once a week.

Simple Past: indicating an action or situation that began and ended in the past at one particular time

Examples: The Captain just <u>went</u> back to his cabin. He <u>was</u> on the bridge a few minutes ago.

He <u>stayed</u> on the bridge from 0830 to 1000.

Regular verbs

He <u>reported</u> it immediately to the Chief Engineer.

He <u>maintained</u> the fire fighting equipment yesterday.

Irregular verbs

He <u>kept</u> the oil-transfer checklist one hour ago.

<u>*Simple Future:*</u>   indicating an action that will happen at one particular time in the future

Examples: The pilot <u>will board</u> the ship in two hours. It <u>will rain</u> tomorrow. I'<u>m going to</u> meet the new cadet later.

It's your turn:

Write the verbs with correct tenses in the blanks.

1. I usually (get) _____ home at five, but today I (get) _____ home at seven.

2. He (live) _____ in the United States for ten years, but now he (live) _____ in Japan.

3. I (call) _____ him last night, but he (be) _____ not at home. His mother (say) _____ he (study) _____ in the library.

4. Today (be) _____ a beautiful day. The sun is shining, and the birds are singing.

5. I (drop) _____ my cup, and the Coffee (spill) _____ on my paints.

6. Water (consist) _____ of hydrogen and oxygen.

7. The ship (be decommissioned) _____ this fall.

8. The ship (be launched) _____ in 1967.

Part Three: Reading

A letter to home: describing life at sea

Recreation Room, picture from EVERGREEN.com

Dear Mom,

How are you? I'm healthy and strong. We have been out at sea for two months. Now we are making our course across the Atlantic. At sea, much of the time is spent maintaining the ship and keeping her equipment in good conditions. There is constant cleaning, painting and repairing work.

Today, I did my morning watch from 0400 to 0800. The Chief Engineer gave me a list of jobs to do. I checked the correct functioning of the main engine and auxiliaries. Everything went smoothly. After dinner, I played chess with my best friend, Andy in the officers' lounge. I won again.

I usually have enough rest, and there are some leisure activities we can do to help us relax. We can do exercise in the fitness room. Sometimes when I am off my duty at night, I like to go to my favorite place on the deck, gazing up into the starry heaven. It is really beautiful and peaceful. If the weather is bad, I watch movies with my shipmates. There are a lot of films on the ship, comedy, musical, horror movies, science fiction, and so on. Yesterday, our captain wanted everyone to watch a safety video. It was about emergency response. In fact, major emergencies at sea are rare. Don't worry about my safety.

Last month when our ship was in port, I went with Andy ashore. He needed to get supplies, and I needed to find some mechanic parts. We went down the winding streets and found a busy square. There were crowds of people surrounding the vendors and street performances. It's an interesting place.

Everything goes pretty well with me. Please take good care of yourself.

love,

Your son

Officers' Lounge, picture from EVERGREEN.com

Reading comprehension:

1. Which department do you think the author may work in?
2. Does the author seem to enjoy his job?
3. What does the author do to relax?
4. What can the crew usually do on board during their leisure time?
5. Why did the author go ashore last month?

Part Four: Exercises

A. Look at the pictures. Circle the persons who may work at the places and describe what the person is doing in each picture.

1. Who may work in this control room under the deck?

    Deck Officers
    Engineer Officers

2. Who may work here on the deck?

    Deck Officers
    Deck Hands

3. Who may work here in the galley?

    Chief Officer
    Chief Cook

4. Who may work here on the bridge?

    Deck Officers
    Engineer Officers

B. Say and Write in English.

1. 我負責甲板部門、船的維修和航行。

_____

2. 我的工作是維護引擎。

_____

3. 船長監督所有部門。

_____

4. 我的班是早上四點到八點，和下午四點到八點。

_____

5. 那位棕髮高個子是誰？

_____

C. Listen and Answer.　🎧 Track 14

Listen to an interview of the captain and answer the following questions:

(　) 1. Which of the following is not the captain's duty?

　　　a) Stand watch.

　　　b) Preparing the Ship's Papers and the documents.

　　　c) Supervising the work done by the crew.

　　　d) Maintaining the ship's log and the records of the ship's movements.

(　) 2. What does the captain think would help to maintain team spirit and atmosphere on board?

　　　a) Being familiar with all the work done by all of the crew members.

　　　b) Keeping on learning new things and skills.

　　　c) Having good daily communication and interactions.

　　　d) Having fun when working with people.

(　) 3. What does the captain's daughter look like?

      a) Her eye color is blue.

      b) She's got short hair.

      c) She's tall and beautiful.

      d) She's got black hair.

(　) 4. What will the captain do after he retires?

      a) He will travel the world on cruise ships with his wife.

      b) He will write a book.

      c) He will teach music.

      d) He will work for a software company.

D. Pair Work : Guess who I'm describing.

Work in a small group. Choose someone in your group and describe his or her physical appearance and personality. Then the rest of the people in the group guess who the person may be.

E. Create a Character Profile.

Work in small group. Pick up a character (Master, chief officer, second officer, chief engineer, bosun, etc.) for creating his/her personal information. Give a background story for the character, and then share your profile in class.

Major information should include:

Name:
Age: (e.g., in his/her 20s, 30s, 40s, 50s)
Nationality/Home town:
Place of birth:
Marital status: (single, engaged, married, divorced)
Family Members & family life: (parents, wife, sons and daughters)
Physical appearance: (hair color, hair style, face shape, body type, etc.)
Personality:
Hobbies/Activities in the leisure time:
Position on board/Job description:

I like fresh food better.

Part One: Food on Board

Conversation 1 : I'm glad that you enjoyed the food aboard.

Scenario: The deck cadet boarded the ship a month ago. He just finished his dinner and came out from the mess room. The food was served in buffet style. The Chief Officer came to chat with him about the food on board.

Mess room, picture from EVERGREEN.com

Pre-listening Questions

    1. What did the cadet pick up for his dinner?

    2. What does the cadet think is a tough task?

Conversation 1 : 🎧 Track 15

Chief Officer: What did you pick up for your dinner?

Cadet: I had some fruit salad, a steak, smoked salmon, sautéed mushrooms, baked potatoes, sausage, with baskets of hot, oven-baked bread. For dessert, I chose yogurt, chocolate and lemon cakes made with real chocolate and freshly squeezed lemon juice. They're delicious!

Chief Officer: You must have been hungry! I'm glad you enjoyed the food aboard. I picked up the smoked salmon too. It tasted really good! The sausage was too spicy for me. The soup today wasn't very good. Did you get any after dinner drinks? They're served on the other serving counter.

Cadet: Yes, I got some cappuccino. Better than what I used to have at Coffee shop.

Chief Officer: You know, when we're out to sea, the highlight of the day is food. Food is such a reward for working hard. One good thing is our menu does not repeat too often. Meals aboard also follow a balanced nutritional structure. The chef even offers calorie-friendly entrees for the sake of health.

Cadet: I totally agree. But I guess feeding all of us must be a tough task since we're all from different parts of the world.

Chief Officer: That's true. It's quite challenging. Our chef needs to be sensitive to the cultural and dietary needs of sailors. Besides, cooking is also confined to season or climate. I'm very proud of our Catering Department. Not only their cooking, but also how they keep a detailed food inventory and get sufficient food and drinks for the expected time away from shore.

Cadet: Now I can see every department aboard is important. I wonder how much food our ship carries when leaving the port.

Chief Officer:	Well, some specialty items might need to be stockpiled. Time in storage for large vessels is longer, but supplies always need to be replenished at each port of call.
Cadet:	I like fresh food better!
Chief Officer:	So do I.

Comprehension Questions : 🎧 Track 16

1. What do most crew members think is a reward for their hard work?
2. What should the chef take into consideration before he prepares meals?
3. Why does the cadet think feeding all of the crew members aboard is a tough task?
4. What else are crew members of the Catering Department responsible for besides cooking?
5. When do they get food supplies?

Express attitude through intonation and pitch 🎧Track 17

Intonation is the way the voice rises or falls during speech.

1. use of rising intonation and high pitch with adjectives or adverbs to express personal preference

   They're de<u>licious</u>!　　It tasted <u>really good</u>!　　I like fresh food <u>better</u>!

2. use of falling intonation and low pitch with adjectives to express personal preference

   It's <u>too spicy</u>.　　The Coffee today isn't <u>very good</u>.

Conversation 2 : In the galley 🎧 Track 18

Scenario: The cadet was passing by the galley. He came in to say hello to the chef.

galley, picture from EVERGREEN.com

Cadet:	Hi, chef. How're you doing?
The Chef:	OK, son. We're getting close to our next port. I'm checking the food inventory. It seems to me we need to get at least 50 gallons of fresh milk, 1000 pounds of seafood, and 100 dozens of eggs in Hong Kong.
Cadet:	Good to hear that we'll get fresh food soon. By the way, I've never been to Hong Kong. How do you like Hong Kong?
The Chef:	OK. It's quite convenient to get fresh food there. I can get good bargains, but I hate the traffic. Recently food costs have risen.
Cadet:	What are inside these packages?
The Chef:	Flour. The largest sacks of flour are far less expensive but contamination and waste are bigger problems when a container must be opened and closed regularly. So I repackaged it. This is a way to minimize waste and spoilage.

Cadet:	Chef, you're so talented! Wait! What smells so good in the ovens?
The Chef:	Ah-ha, turkeys with my great grandmother's secret recipe.
Cadet:	Turkey? That reminds me of the Thanksgiving Day at home. I always helped my mom to chop and mix spices together. Did you put some in the stuffing?
The Chef:	Yes, I did. Garlic, peppers and more. How did you like the food last night?
Cadet:	Everything was delicious. I started with green salad which was very fresh. Then I tried BBQ ribs. They're pretty tender and the sauce was terrific. I had side dishes until I felt stuffed and couldn't have more.
The Chef:	You really pleased me! We've got a lot of labor to do on board. We'll need enough energy to get our work done.
Cadet:	That's just what I think.

Comprehension Questions : 🎧 Track 19

1. What food will they pick up in the next port?
2. Why did the Chef repackage flour?
3. What is on the menu for tonight's dinner?
4. What did the cadet think of the BBQ ribs he had last night?
5. What do the cadet and the chef both agree on?

Part Two: Grammar, Language and Cultural Tips

A. Agreement & Disagreement

Agreeing with someone

> That's true.
>
> Quite right.
>
> Point taken.
>
> That's just what I think.
>
> I feel the same way.
>
> So do/am I.
>
> I totally agree. (I agree with you entirely.)

Disagreeing with someone or an argument

> I hate to disagree with you, but…
>
> I'm afraid I disagree.
>
> I can't possibly accept that.
>
> That's not the same thing at all.
>
> But that's different.

Statement	*Your opinion*
1. The Italian restaurants here are very expensive. _____	
2. I don't like chocolate cakes because all of them are too sweet. _____	

B. Preferences

Questions you may ask:

How do you like Hong Kong?
What do you think of Hong Kong?
Do you like Hong Kong?

Answers you may give:

I love it! It's exciting.
I really like it.

How do you like the food?
What do you think of the food?
Do you like the food?

It's great! It's fantastic!
It's OK.
It's not bad.

Responses you may give:

So do I.
Me, too.

Or answers you may give:

I hate it. It's noisy.
I can't stand it.
I don't like it at all.
I don't really like it.

Or responses you may give:

Neither do I.
Neither can I.
Me, neither.

Or answers you may give:

I'm not sure. I've never been there.
I'm not sure. I've never tried it before.

It's your turn:

Do you like spicy food? _____

What do you think of Italian food? _____

How do you like chocolate cakes? _____

C. Ordering food at restaurant 🎧 **Track 20**

Example A

Waiter:	May I take your order now?
Customer:	Yes. I'd like the fried chicken.
Waiter:	What would you like with your chicken, a baked potato or French fries?
Customer:	French fries, please.
Waiter:	What would you like to drink? Tea or Coffee?
Customer:	Tea will be fine.

(The customer has done his eating.)

Waiter:	Do you want anything else?
Customer:	No, thanks. Check, please.

Example B

Waitress:	What would you like, sir?
Customer:	I haven't decided yet. What's today's special?
Waitress:	Roast beef with green salad.
Customer:	That sounds good. I'll have it, please.
Waitress:	What kind of dressing would you like?
Customer:	Thousand Island, please.
Waitress:	Would you care for some dessert?
Customer:	No, thank you.

It's your turn to order your meal with a partner. Work out your own dialogue by using the following menu.

Menu

Appetizer
  Green Salad
  Seafood Cocktail
  Soup of the Day

Main Course/Entree
  BBQ Ribs with baked potatoes
  Roast Beef with fried rice
  Chicken Chow Mein

Side dishes
  French fries
  Onion rings
  Baked potatoes

Dessert
  Vanilla Ice Cream
  Classic Cheese Cake
  Lemon Cake

Beverages
  Herbal Tea
  American Coffee
  Cappuccino

Exercise: Complete the following conversation.

Waiter: Good evening.

Bill: I made a _____ for two under the name Bill Johnson.

Waiter: Yes. Come this way, please.

         Here is our _____ . Would you like something to drink before you _____ ?

Bill: Sparkling mineral water, please.

Tom: Me too.

(The waiter came back.)

Waiter: Sparkling mineral water. Are you ready to order now, or should I come back later to _____ your order?

Bill: This is our first time here. Could you _____ us order?

Waiter: Sure. We have a great set meal. It comes with starter, main course, dessert and beverage. The selections for _____ are steamed asparagus and spicy chicken legs.

Tom: I'd like to have the spicy chicken legs.

Bill: I don't like spicy food. Steamed asparagus for me.

Waiter: What would you like for your _____ ? Is there anything you don't particularly like?

Bill: I am _____ to crab and shrimps.

Tom: I don't eat beef. I like seafood.

Waiter: We have very fresh lobsters today. Filet mignon is very popular here. It's very tender.

Tom: Lobster sounds good to me.

Bill: I'll have filet mignon, medium.

Waiter: And _____ after your meal? Lemon cake or tiramisu?

Bill: I'd like tiramisu and Earl Grey tea, please.

Tom: Lemon cake.

Waiter: All right. I will _____ your order to the kitchen.

(After they finished eating…)

Bill:	Could we get the _____ , please?
Waiter:	Would you like separate checks?
Bill:	Yes, we're going Dutch, thanks.

D. Word Study: Any and Some

"some" in positive statement, and "any" in negative statement:

1. I had some fruit salad.
2. I didn't have any fruit salad.
3. I have some friends in the United States.
4. I don't have any friends in the United States.
5. Do you have any money?

   Yes, I have some./No, I don't have any.

"any" in the "if or whether" clause:

6. If you have any questions, don't be afraid to ask.
7. I doubt whether he has any friends here.

"some" in the question form with an understanding that the answer will be positive:

8. Did you put some spices in the soup? It tastes more delicious. Yes, I did.
9. Would you like to have some more tea? Yes, thank you.

E. Nouns

Count Nouns

Singular: a chart, a fire extinguisher, an axe, an announcement, a dish, a tomato, a foot, a man, a child

Plural: charts, fire extinguishers, axes, announcements, dishes, tomatoes, feet, men, children

* A few and few are used with plural count nouns.

e.g., a few friends (with a positive idea, referred to some friends)

few friends (with a negative idea, referred almost no friends)

Non-count Nouns

information, equipment, luggage, news, advice, evidence, work, money, weather, water, music, scenery, traffic, food, fruit, salt, rice, sugar, flour, meat, pepper, butter, bread, milk, tea, enjoyment, happiness, fun, sadness, courage, honesty, luck, violence, poverty, wealth

* a piece of information/equipment/luggage/furniture/news/advice

* a cup of tea, a glass of milk

* weight measure: a pound of food, fruit, salt, rice, meat, sugar, flour

two pounds of food, fruit, salt, rice, meat, sugar, flour

* liquid measure : a quarter/pint/gallon of milk, oil, etc.

* a little money (with a positive idea, referred to some money)

little money (with a negative idea, referred almost no money)

* **A lot of/lots of and plenty of can be used to modify count and non-count nouns.**

I have a lot of work to do. You have plenty of time to finish it.

I have a lot of friends. Plenty of the men are here now.

Fill in with a suitable word to complete the sentence.

1. The captain just made _____ announcement.

2. He gave me _____ advice.

3. He carried _____ luggage.

4. He has _____ work to do tonight.

5. This book contains _____ information.

6. I brought 6 _____ of sugar.

F. Report damage to food cargoes

There are different types of cargoes: bulk cargo and general cargo. Bulk cargo may have cargo in liquid form like oil or dry things like grain, iron-ore, coal, sugar, and so on. These goods are carried in tankers or holds. General cargo carrues a variety of goods packed separately in bags, bales, cases or steel drums and are usually put in containers. Therefore, vessels have stowage plans to load or discharge the cargoes.

Various kinds of food like dairy products, tea, rice, tobacco, meat, and fruit are among the cargoes carried by ship. Some of them need to be kept in refrigerated holds with correct temperature. An official inspection report is needed to tell about the quantity and condition of the food for the discharge of food from a ship. The report also covers causes of food damage in addition to the quantity of the losses. Food damage may take place because of different reasons.

1. Inadequate Packaging

   In this case, damage is not caused by improper handling during shipping or discharge, but results from inadequate packaging of the food in the country of origin. The report needs to document the information of type of food, package size, and description of packaging deficiencies.

2. Marine Damage

   There are several types of damage: mold/sweat because of damp storage conditions, condensation or improper ventilation; infestation because of holds not thoroughly cleaned and fumigated before loading or improper segregation of infested food; sea water damage or fresh water damages because of leak; cut/ torn containers because of improper handling while loading or discharging; contamination.

3. Damages during Discharge at the Port

It could happen before discharge from ship, during discharge from ship to port storage area, and during repackaging at the dock or port storage area.

4. Sweepings

Sweepings are spillages collected in the ship's holds, collected from torn bags, or collected after repacking. The total weight of the sweepings or the number of units needs to be reported.

5. Infestation

The inspector needs to get a sample of bags examined for possible insect infestations. If the sample shows the shipment to be infested, then the report needs to tell the amount of the original shipment, the amount able to be repackaged, and the amount that may be unfit.

Part Three: Reading

Dining on the Cruise Ship

Cruise fare in fact includes the top two expenses of traveling —accommodation and food. Guests may choose to live in a deluxe suite or an inside room with no windows to the outside, depending on their budgets. One of the primary selling points of a cruise ship is a dining experience that is both entertaining and delicious. Today, every cruise line is constantly trying to improve its dining programs. More luxurious dining rooms and restaurants are established by celebrity chefs. Cruisers can enjoy the special ambience and sociable atmosphere of the main dining rooms. They may also choose to dine in a help-yourself buffet or a Coffee in a more casual way. Different kinds of options are available for them to reserve tables or dining time. These different dining styles and options ensure cruisers an enjoyable trip.

Cruisers can have most of the food for free unless some is specified explicitly charged. Water, tea, and Coffee are provided as much as they want. Alcoholic drinks and fruit punch may be billed to guest's account. Breakfast tends to be the most mundane affair of the day and all dining options serve regular foods like French toast, scrambled eggs, bacon, porridge, cereal, fruits, sausages, and made to order omelets. For most cruisers, breakfast and lunch are casual affairs while dinner is more formal. Cruisers can dress up and indulge in the fine dining experience at captain's party. They can never be too overdressed on those nights.

Write T for true or F for false for each of the following statements.

(　) 1. Cruisers need to pay extra money for accommodation and food on cruise ships.

(　) 2. Cruise lines make great efforts in providing cruisers good dining experiences.

(　) 3. All the food and drinks on board are free.

(　) 4. Guests can order omelets according to their preferences for dinner.

(　) 5. Guests are required to dress themselves formally for having meals on board.

Part Four: More Exercises

A. Dictation. 🎧 Track 21

1. _____

2. _____

3. _____

4. _____

B. Listen and Circle. 🎧 Track 22

Jason is ordering food at a restaurant. A waitress is helping. Listen to their conversation and circle the correct answers.

1. Jason is ordering food for his (breakfast/lunch/dinner).

2. What kind of pancakes will Jason have? (classic/fruit/chocolate).

3. What beverage will Jason have? (orange/apple /tomato)

4. What else will Jason have? (omelets/bacon/eggs)

C. Fill in the blank.

1. A: What did you have for appetizer? B: I had _____ fruit salad.

2. A: Did you try the cakes?   B: No, I didn't have _____ dessert.

3. A: I want to go to the supermarket. B: Could you get a _____ milk and 2 _____ of sugar for me?

4. A: He is a new comer here. Where can he possibly go? B: I can't figure it out. He has _____ friends here.

D. Discuss with your group members about the food in your school cafeteria. Tell what you agree and disagree.

E. Internet search: Find 3 kinds of vegetables and 4 kinds of fruit and share how to say them in English with your partner.

F. Create a new menu of your restaurant of any kind.

<table>
<tr><td>Unit
4</td><td># What kind of vessel is it?</td></tr>
</table>

Part One: Types of Vessels

Multi-Deck Cargo

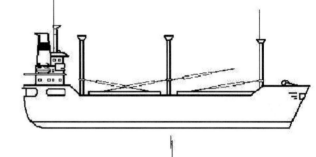

Commercial Fishing Boat

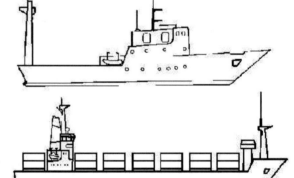

Container Ship

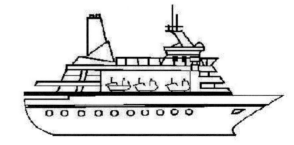

Cruise Ship

Conversation 1 : How are vessels classified?

Scenario: Keiko, Jack and the Captain are discussing types of vessels.

Pre-Listening Questions:

1. How can a vessel be classified?
2. What kind of vessel is a tug boat?

Conversation 1 : 🎧 Track 23

Keiko:	Captain, how are vessels classified?
Captain:	Generally speaking, a vessel can be classified according to the purpose it serves. For example, vessels designed to transport cargo or passengers, are both called merchant ships.
Jack:	Passenger ships like ferries or liners carry passengers and their vehicles on a prearranged route.
Captain:	Yes. Other merchant ships like general cargo ship and the open freighter carry different kinds of cargo.
Jack:	Then there are also other ships providing assistance and service.

Captain:	Yes, they're called special purpose vessels, like a tug boat, a salvage vessel, or a fireboat.
Keiko:	What is a tug boat for?
Captain:	A tug boat is a vessel that assists other vessels with entering or leaving a port.
Jack:	A salvage vessel rescues other ships.
Captain:	That's right.
Keiko:	How about fishing boats? Are they also special purpose vessels?
Jack:	Yes, they are.

Comprehension Questions : 🎧 Track 24

1. What do ferries or liners carry?
2. What do cargo ships and the open freighters carry?
3. What is a tug boat for?
4. What is a salvage vessel for?
5. What kind of vessel is a fishing boat?

Conversation 2 : Vessel Information 🎧 Track 25

Scenario: Jack is reading the newspaper. Then Keiko and Jack are talking about some vessel information.

Keiko:	Anything new?
Jack:	Here's an interesting news report. It says, "Three Queen ships lined up in front of the Statue of Liberty for a special event yesterday. At eight in the evening, they were slowly moving across New York Harbor under a shower of fireworks."
Keiko:	Wait! What are the three Queen ships?
Jack:	The Queen Mary 2, Queen Elizabeth 2 and the new Queen Victoria.
Keiko:	Oh, the Queen Elizabeth 2! It's one of the world's most famous cruise ships. It says that she was launched in 1967.
Jack:	That's right. And she is the longest-serving vessel of her shipping company. But it'll be decommissioned this fall.
Keiko:	What would happen to it?
Jack:	Well, it's sold for US$100 million to Dubai World. So, it'll become a floating five-star hotel in Dubai.
Keiko:	Really? Great!
Jack:	Queen Mary 2 is also a wonderful ocean liner. It was once the longest, widest and tallest passenger ship ever built.
Keiko:	Is it very old, too?
Jack:	No, not really. It was constructed in 2003. There're 15 restaurants and bars, five swimming pools, a casino, a ballroom, a theatre, and a planetarium on board.
Keiko:	No kidding? That's amazing!
Jack:	But Queen Victoria is more gorgeous than Queen Mary 2. It has a 6,000-volume, two-deck-high library, a light-filled spa, a casino, a museum, and a show lounge…
Keiko:	Oh! I need to save money. I want to go on a vacation on it some day.

Comprehension Questions : 🎧 Track 26

1. Where did the three queen ships meet?
2. When was the Queen Elizabeth 2 launched?
3. Which ship will be decommissioned this fall?
4. What will the Queen Elizabeth 2 become after this fall?
5. Which ship of the three was once the longest, widest and tallest passenger ship ever built?
6. Which ship's facilities are more gorgeous than the other two?
7. What kind of vessels are the three queen ships?

Pronunciation: Word Stress 🎧 Track 27

● ·	· ●	· ● ·	· · ●
merchant	design	assistance	prearranged
vessel	transport	according	
salvage	hotel	casino	
firework	museum	amazing	
floating		vacation	
longest			
ocean			
lounge			

· · ● · ·

decommissioned

planetarium

Part Two: Grammar, Cultural and Language Tips

A. The International Code of Signals 🎧 Track 28

The spoken words are assigned as codes for letters A to Z, used by vessels during transmission of a message. The codes are from an international system of signals and codes called *The International Code of Signals*. In maritime context, people use them to clarify information in communication for the purpose of preventing confusion. For example, the word ("Army" would be "Alfa Romeo Mike Yankee" when spelled in the phonetic alphabet.

A	Alfa	**N**	November
B	Bravo	**O**	Oscar
C	Charlie	**P**	Papa
D	Delta	**Q**	Quebec
E	Echo	**R**	Romeo
F	Foxtrot	**S**	Sierra
G	Golf	**T**	Tango
H	Hotel	**U**	Uniform
I	India	**V**	Victor
J	Juliet	**W**	Whisky
K	Kilo	**X**	X-ray
L	Lima	**Y**	Yankee
M	Mike	**Z**	Zulu

Use the spelling of letters to give vessel's name

Example 1:

Scenario: Christina, a Ro-Ro and passenger ship, is contacting Shanghai station. Its call sign is 3 FKX8.

Christina: Shanghai station, Shanghai station. This is Christina, Calling on three, one, nine, five kilohertz. How do you read me? Over.

Shanghai Station: Christina, this is Shanghai Station. I read you excellent. Spell the name of your vessel, please.

Christina: My vessel name is Christina. Charlie Hotel Romeo India Sierra Tango India November Alfa, over.

Shanghai Station: Your call sign, please.

Christina: 3 Foxtrot Kilo X-ray 8, over.

Shanghai Station: Thank you, sir.

Practice: Your turn to contact Shanghai station. Your ship name is MSC Bettina

Use the spelling of letters to give your name in a marine context

Scenario: Chief Mate is meeting a new AB (Able Seamen).

Chief Mate: Welcome on board. I am the Chief Mate.

AB: Good morning, Chief. I am the new AB.

Chief Mate: What's your name?

AB: My first name is Eric. Echo Romeo India Charlie My family name is Parker. Papa Alpha Romeo Kilo Echo Romeo.

Chief Mate: Do you have your seaman's book and passport?

AB: Yes. Here you are, Chief.

Chief Mate: Where are you from?

AB: I'm from Chicago, United States.

Chief Mate: Your date of birth?

AB: March 4th, 1985.

Chief Mate: Where did you work before?

AB: I worked as an OS (Ordinary Seamen) on the Maria, a Reefer, for 3 years.

Good. I will guide you to meet the Bosun. He will take you to your cabin and then meet the captain.

AB: Thank you, Chief.

B. The Passive of verbs in grammar

Active	*Passive*
Mary usually helps Kevin.	Kevin is usually helped by Mary.
How do we classify vessels?	A vessel can be classified according to her mission.
We call them merchant ships.	They are called merchant ships.
They built the ship in 1790.	The ship was built in 1970.
His friend will help him.	He will be helped by his friend.

Practice: Your turn to complete the sentences

1. Lots of people will (miss) _____ Queen Elizabeth 2.

2. Queen Elizabeth 2 (sell) _____ for US $ 100 million last year.

3. Queen Elizabeth 2 will (decommission) _____ this fall.

4. Queen Mary 2 (construct) _____ in 2003.

5. Queen Elizabeth 2 will (become) _____ a floating five-star hotel.

6. The vessel _____ (register) in Panama.

7. The vessel _____ (hit) the headlines.

C. Comparative and superlative forms of adjectives

Original adjective	Comparative adjective	Superlative adjectives
One-syllable adjectives		
long	longer	the longest
wide	wider	the widest
tall	taller	the tallest
large	larger	the largest
Two-or-more syllable adjectives		
famous	more famous	the most famous
beautiful	more beautiful	the most beautiful

Two-syllable adjectives that end in −y

busy	busier	the busiest
early	earlier	the earliest

Irregular forms of adjectives

good	better	the best
bad	worse	the worst
little	less	the least
far	farther	the farthest

Examples:

The Queen Mary 2 is longer than the Queen Elizabeth 2.

The Queen Mary 2 was once the longest, widest and tallest passenger ship ever built.

Practice: Your turn to complete the sentences

1. Queen Mary 2 is (large) _____ than Queen Elizabeth 2.
2. It is (little) _____ than three nautical miles from here to the shore.
3. The weather is getting (good) _____ .
4. I walked 5 miles, but Tom walked only 3 miles. I walked (far) _____ than he did.

D. Accommodation at sea and on land

Cabins (or staterooms) on ships are all air-conditioned akin to hotel rooms although they are typically smaller. In the accommodation area of the cargo ships, officers usually have their private cabins on the upper decks with facilities like a Coffee table, a writing desk, a refrigerator, a bed, and a private bathroom. Cabins can vary from ship to ship. Generally speaking, there are inside cabins and outside cabins. Inside cabins are the rooms with no window to the outside. Outside cabins will have a window or porthole (a round window) with good natural light.

On cruise ships, cabins fall into more different types: inside, outside, balcony, and luxurious suites. Ample area is offered for the cruisers to enjoy the sea going experience. Balcony cabins give additional private outside space for passengers to step outside for enjoying the ocean view without going up to a public deck. Suites are larger cabins, often with separate lounge and sleeping areas. You may find a in-cabin bar with tea and Coffee making facilities and a refrigerator in the rooms. The services of a personal cabin steward are offered to look after your every need from early morning until late evening. Most cruise lines put their nicest cabins to the highest decks, usually below the pool deck for a large window or balcony. However, the higher decks and cabins at the very forward or aft of the ship tend to rock and roll the most.

Seafarers also have opportunities to find a place to stay on land. The most common types of accommodation for them to choose are: guest house, hostel, motel, and hotel. It depends on their budgets. They can call or book a room through the Internet. The following is an example of making a reservation over the telephone.

Hotel Clerk: Sunny Hotel. May I help you?

Traveler: Yes, my name is Peter Dickson. I'd like to make a reservation from March 4th to 7th. Do you have any vacancies?

Hotel Clerk: Yes, we do have some. How many will there be in your party?

Traveler: Just one. I'd like to have a single room. How much is the nightly rate?

Hotel Clerk: You have two options. One is more quite with a mountain view. For the dates you'll be staying, it's US$105 per night. And the other one facing the street is US$ 95. Both include breakfast.

Traveler: Do you offer a discount to the members of FUN Club?

Hotel Clerk: No, sorry. We don't have that program any more since it is high season now.

Traveler: OK. I will book the one facing the street.

Hotel Clerk: May I get the information from you for the reservation? Your name again, and your credit card information?

E. Facilities on ships

The crew's and passengers' needs are taken into good consideration in addition to the safety sake. We can find common areas like lounge, mess room/hall, and recreation rooms on board. The crew and passengers may have access to watch movies, play cards or other games, sing karaoke in the lounge, play table tennis, or use basic equipment like weights in a small gym or a recreation room. There are probably only 6-12 people on a cargo ship, so the units are usually smaller. On container ships, you may find a half basketball court. Comparing to them, cruise ships have more sport and leisure faculties for spectacular entertainment.

F. Size of Ship

Gross tonnage (GRT) is calculated by measuring a ship's volume (from keel to funnel, to the outside of the hull framing). It is used to determine things in safety rules, registration fees, and port dues etc. It is also used to talk about the size of passenger ships and fishing ships.

Deadweight (DWT) is a measure of how much weight a ship is carrying or can safely carry. It is the sum of the weights of cargo, fuel, fresh water, ballast water, provisions, passengers, and crews. The size of a cargo vessel is described by DWT.

Net tonnage (NT) is calculated by measuring a ship's internal volume of the ship's cargo spaces.

Lightship, lightweight or light displacement measures the actual weight of the ship with no fuel, passengers, cargo, water, etc. on board。

Part Three: Reading

Vessels and Cargoes

Most merchant ships are designed to carry dry cargo, liquid cargo, or both. Bulk, multi-deck, container, refrigerated and roll on-roll off (Ro-Ro) are dry cargo carriers.

They transport unpackaged bulk cargo such as chemicals, grain, coal, iron ore, timber, and cement. Reefers are short for refrigerated containers to carry diary, fruit, vegetables, etc. They can keep temperatures anywhere from room temperature to -30 degree. Bulkers make up about a third of the world's merchant fleet. New Liquefied Natural Gas (LNG) carriers, growing rapidly, continue to be built to carry gas stored in a liquid state. Other vessels carrying liquid cargo are oil tankers and chemical carriers. Oil, Bulk, Ore (OBO) carries both dry and liquid cargo like oil, bulk, and ore.

Cargo ships can operate as liners or tramps. Any member of the public may check information of liners from a regularly published schedule of ports about their routes and timetable. Ships which operate as tramps do not sail on regular routes. This is private business arranged between the shipper and receiver. It is facilitated by the vessel owners or operators, who offer their vessels for hire to carry cargo to any suitable port in the world.

Passenger ships are fewer in number and type than cargo ships. Ferries and other liner are the most common type of passenger ship. However, cruise ships are very popular for pleasure voyages nowadays. Passenger ships usually operate as liners on regular routes and a fixed timetable. People can find their arrival and departure time and even book seats on the Internet.

Container ship, picture from EVERGREEN MARINE CORP.

Answer the following questions based on the reading text.

1. What do bulk carriers and container ships usually carry?
2. What kind of ships usually carries liquid cargo?
3. What kind of ships usually carries gas stored in a liquid state?
4. How do cargo ships operate?
5. Where can people find the arrival and departure time of passenger ships?

Vocabulary Study: Put the words in the categories.

bulker

carrier

chemicals

cement

grain

coal

cruises

ferries

gas

oil tankers

liners

iron ore

Ro-Ro

vessel

Ship	Cargo

Part Four: More Exercises

A. Matching

Description of words   Words to choose

( )1. a trip of a vessel   a) fuel oil

( )2. opposite of load   b) voyage

( )3. destination of discharging cargo   c) fragile cargo

( )4. lifting and moving heavy weights   d) ferry

( )5. a kind of refined products   f) perishable cargo

( )6. a type of passenger ship   g) port of delivery

( )7. goods which are easy to break   h) discharge

( )8. a place where fruit and meat need to be put in   i) refrigerated holds

                                                       j) derrick

B. Complete the following sentences.

1. Vessels designed to _____ cargo or passengers or both are called ____ _____ ships.

2. A vessel can be classified _____ to the purpose it serves or the cargo it carries.

3. Passenger ships are _____ in number and type than cargo ships.

4. Passenger ships like _____ or liners carry passengers and their vehicles on a _____ route.

5. _____ ships are very popular for pleasure voyages nowadays.

6. The Queen Elizabeth 2 is the longest-serving vessel. It was _____ in 1967 but soon will be _____ and become a _____ five-star hotel near the shore of Dubai.

7. Fruit and meat need to be put in _____ holds.

C. Listen to the CD and complete the vessel information based on what you hear. 🎧 **Track 29**

Ship's name	
Flag	
Vessel type	
Length overall	
Extreme breadth	
Gross tonnage	
Maximum draft	
Maximum speed	
DWT(Dead weight)	
Date of Debut	

D. Internet search: Find a vessel, describe the vessel type and facilities on board, and share in class.

E. Pair Work. Ask your partner the information you need in order to fill in your chart.

Student A's chart:

Ship's name		MSC Bettina
Call sign	9V9129	
Flag	Singapore	
Date of build	2011	
Vessel type		Container Ship
Gross tonnage		151559
Length overall	362m	
Extreme breadth	65 m	

Student B's chart:

Ship's name	Vale Italia	
Call sign		HPFG
Flag		Panama
Date of build		1010
Vessel type	Bulk Carrier	
Gross tonnage	200000	
Length overall		366 m
Extreme breadth		52 m

Unit 5

Where is the captain's cabin?

Part One: Places and Equipment on Board

Conversation 1 : What are the major rooms on this ship?

Scenario: Carlos is showing Keiko around on the ship. They are on the main deck.

galley, picture from EVERGREEN MARINE CORP.

Pre-Listening Questions:

1. What room are they visiting?
2. What rooms are below the main deck?

Conversation 1 : 🎧 **Track 30**

Carlos: Ovens, freezers, a food disposer, and a dishwasher. We have almost everything that a big restaurant on land has.

Keiko: Wow, stainless steel food service equipment! Everything in this kitchen is neat.

Carlos: On board, we call it the galley, and the place we have meals is the mess room.

Keiko: That's interesting. Do you have other names on the ship that differ from what we call on land?

Carlos: Um, "head". That's the name for toilet on the ship. And "bunk", is bed on a ship.

Keiko: Are all the major rooms on the main deck?

Carlos: Rooms like the bridge, radio room, laundry, and cabins are all on the main deck, but the engine room and pump room are below deck.

Keiko: Why are they below the deck?

Carlos: The machines to run the ship are very heavy, so they are placed deep in the hull for good balance.

Keiko: That makes sense. Which deck is the bridge on?

Carlos: It's on the upper deck, above the captain's cabin. We're one level below it now.

Keiko: This ship is huge. There are so many rooms and ladders.

Carlos: Follow me down the corridor to the end. You'll see the laundry room. To the right of it is the chief engineer's cabin.

Keiko: Where is the captain's cabin?

Carlos: It's next to the chief officer's cabin.

Keiko: I'll probably get lost without you. I'd better follow you closely.

Comprehension Questions : 🎧 Track 31

1. What is the galley for?
2. Where does the crew have meals?
3. What rooms are under deck? Why?
4. What rooms are at the end of the corridor?
5. Where is the captain's cabin?

Conversation 2 : What are these gears and cables for? 🎧 Track 32

Scenario: Keiko and Carlos are chatting at the fore end of the ship.

Keiko: This is the stern, right?

Carlos: No, this is the forecastle. This makes the bow higher, so the ship can ride more easily in deep seas. We have the mooring equipment here, like the windlass, anchors, cables, wires and hawsers.

Keiko: What is the windlass for?

Carlos: Windlass is a machine for pulling or moving mooring lines. We use it for handling the anchor cables and the hawsers. They are always located at the bow of the ship.

Keiko: To tie the ship to the quay?

Carlos: Yes. Now we're standing to the right side of the vessel, facing the bow. This is called the starboard side.

Keiko: How about the left side?

Carlos: The port side.

Keiko: Facing back to the stern, isn't that one the navigating bridge?

Carlos: Yes. The navigating bridge is the room from which the ship is controlled. The front part of it is the wheelhouse.

Keiko: Wheelhouse? You mean where the wheel and compass are?

Carlos: Yes, there're the steering wheel, radar and other aid controls.

Mooring winches are used for securing a ship to the berth.

Windlass is used to heave up or lower anchor and mooring lines.

the helm or steering wheel

Comprehension Questions : 🎧 Track 33

1. Where are the windlass and the other mooring gear located?

2. What is the windlass for?

3. What do people call the left side of the vessel?

4. What room is the ship controlled from?

5. What equipment will you see in the wheelhouse?

Pronunciation: 🎧 Track 34

Vowels		
[e]	**[ɛ]**	**[æ]**
major	deck	cabin
place	messroom	galley
same	engine	master
radio	heavy	balance
	many	
	level	

Part Two: Grammar, Language and Cultural Tips

A. Asking for and give directions on land

☞ Asking for directions

Ask in a direct way:

1. Where's the nearest subway station?

2. How do I get from here to the market place?

Ask in an indirect way (more polite):

1. Would you know where the nearest subway station is?

2. I wonder if you could tell me where the market place is.

3. Could you tell me where the Central Station is?

☞ Giving directions:

1. Go down the corridor to the end.

2. Go straight ahead.

3. Go a little further.

4. Turn right.

5. Turn left.

6. Go straight for one block (a building or group of buildings built between two streets).

Read the map and complete the sentences.

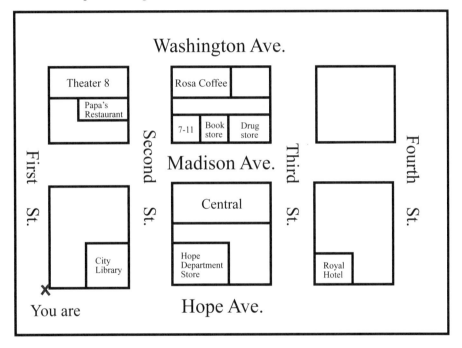

1. Where is Theater 8? Theater 8 is _____ Washington Ave.

2. Where is City Library? It is _____ the end of the block.

3. Where can I find a bookstore? There is one _____ 7-11 and the drug-store.

4. Rosa Coffee is _____ from Theater 8. It's right _____ the corner.

5. Papa's Restaurant is _____ to Theater 8.

6. How do I get to Papa's Restaurant ? Go to the corner and turn _____.
   Go _____ for one block _____ the street and go a little
   further. You will see it.

7. How do I get to Royal Hotel? Go down Hope Ave. for _____ blocks
   and cross Third St..
   It's on your left. You can't miss it!

B. Prepositions of Place

"At" is used with something seen as a point in space, or an intended aim.

   Example: He was standing <u>at</u> the end of the corridor.

"Above" means on a higher level.

   Example: Bridge is <u>above</u> the engine room.

"On" is used with reference to a line or surface.

   Example: The ship stayed <u>on</u> course. The mess room is <u>on</u> Deck 4.

"Over" implies a direct vertical relationship.

   Example: The helicopter hovered <u>over</u> the ship.

"In" means something is within or inside.

   Example: The engine room <u>is</u> in the hull.

"Below" refers to something in or on a lower place/level than the object.

   Example: The captain's cabin is one level <u>below</u>.

"Under" implies something is directly below or lower in rank than another.

   Example: The Log book is <u>under</u> the chart.

Describing a moving ship:

   The cargo ship is outbound <u>from</u> Keelung Harbor. It is moving along the course
of the fairway.

   The cruise ship was seen crossing <u>from</u> Naha port.

C. Describing Locations

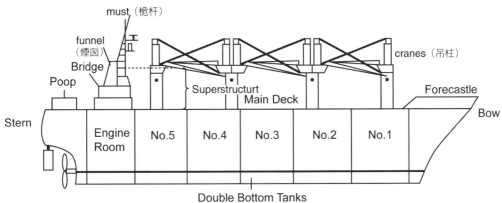

1. The superstructure is placed above the main deck in the stern.

2. Monkey Island is located at the top most accessible height, above the bridge.

3. The mooring gear and windlass are located in the bow of the ship.

4. The forecastle is an elevated platform at the foremost end of the ship.

5. The engine room is below the main deck at the aft of the ship.

6. No. 3 hold is forward of No. 4 hold.

7. The space between the holds and the bottom of the hull contains bottom tanks.

8. Every ship has designated muster stations on the open decks, which are the meeting points during emergencies.

Useful Expressions of describing locations

Something	+	is located is found is positioned is placed	+	on above on top of below or one level below next to the at berth No.2 aft of forward of

Others:

☞ **To the right/left of the ~is~.**

　　To the right of the galley is the mess room.

☞ **past the ~, on the right**

　　The shoe store is past the post office, on your right.

☞ **between ~ and**

A X B

‾X‾ is between ‾A‾ and ‾B‾

☞ ‾X‾ is next to the ‾A/B‾

D. Equipment in a Place

☞ The ship magnetic compass is usually housed on the 'monkey island' above the navigating bridge, so a helmsman can easily read the compass when he is steering the ship.

☞ There is a large dishwasher in the galley.

☞ The steering wheel, radar and other aid controls are in the wheelhouse.

☞ You can find fire extinguishers in the life boats.

E. Simple Present vs. Present Progressive

Simple present: This tense expresses an event or a situation that exists always or usually habitually.

Present progressive: This tense gives the idea that an action is only in progress at the present time.

Simple present	*Present progressive*
We <u>call</u> it the galley.	We<u>'re calling</u> the shore station.
I <u>go to</u> the fit center two times a week.	I <u>am working</u> out in the fit center right now.
He <u>stands</u> a morning watch.	We <u>are standing</u> to the right side of the vessel now.

It's your turn:

1. He went to sleep at 10:00 p.m.. It's 11:00 p.m. right now, and he is still (sleep) _____ .

2. John and Mary go to the same class. They (talk) _____ on the phone about today's homework right now.

3. I need an umbrella before leaving because it (rain) _____ outside.

Part Three: Reading

Read the following passage and sketch a cargo ship based on what you read.

Take this cargo ship as an example. There are some terms describing the parts of the vessel. The breath of a ship at the widest point is called beam. Amidships divides the ship into two main parts. Forward is the front part of the ship. Aft is towards the back part of a boat. Bow or stem is the front end and stern is the back end of a ship. The forecastle is a raised part of the fore deck near the bow, and the poop deck, the raised floor level at the end, is located aft. The funnel of this ship is in the aft. Along the full length of the ship from stem to stern is called fore and aft or Length of Overall(LOA). Across the ship from side to side is athwart. For example, we can describe that a fishing boat is sailing athwart our path. （橫越我們的航道）Facing toward the bow, you see the port side on the left and the starboard side on the right side of the ship. To report the location of the lifeboats on board, we can say the lifeboats of the ship are placed both on the port side amidships and the starboard side amidships.

To report a tug's or other object's position from this cargo ship, we can use the following terms:

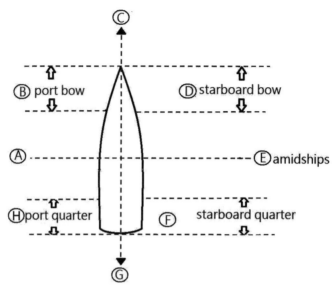

Tug A is off the port beam.

Tug B is off the port bow.

Tug C is ahead.

Tug D is off the starboard bow.

Tug E is off the starboard beam.

Tug F is off the starboard quarter.

Tug G is astern.

Tug H is off the port quarter.

Comprehension Questions

1. Where is the bow? _____

2. Where is the stern? _____

3. What do we call the left side of a ship? _____

4. What do we call the right side of a ship? _____

5. What do we call the full length of the ship from stem to stern? _____

6. What do we call sailing across the ship from side to side? _____

Part Four: More Exercises

A. Say and Write in English

1. 艦橋在哪一層甲板上？

_____

2. 走廊走到底，再右轉。

_____

3. 廚房在下一層。

_____

4. 它們位於船首。

_____

5. 裡面有舵、雷達和其他輔助控制器。

_____

6. 船首樓頂甲板有繫泊設備。

_____

7. 絞盤機用來拉或移動大纜。

_____

8. 引擎室在船的後半部。

_____

9. 拖船在右舷船尾。

_____

10. 在角落右轉直走。

_____

11. 走加油站前面的行人穿越道，然後過馬路。

_____

12. 圖書館在博物館對面。

_____

13. 戲院在藥妝店和旅館中間。

_____

14. 沿這條路走，銀行就在你的正前方。

_____

15. 經過公園，你就會看到市政廳。

_____

16. 火車站怎麼走？

_____

B. Listen to three conversations and find out the locations on the map. 🎧 Track 35

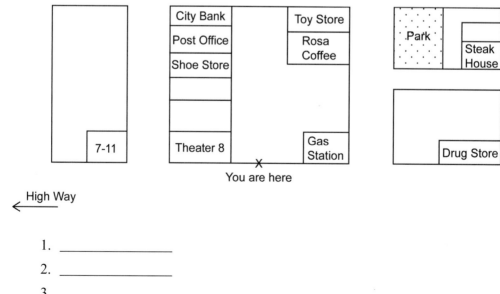

1. _____

2. _____

3. _____

C. Answer questions

Answer questions 1-2 based on the picture.

1. Where is Number 3 hold? _____

hold 4	Engine Room	hold 3	hold 2	hold 1	Forecastle

2. Where is the Number 4 hold? _____

hold 4	Engine Room	hold 3	hold 2	hold 1	Forecastle

3. Where is the forecastle? _____

4. What is fore and aft? _____

D. Word Search

Find 7 words which are hidden in this puzzle.

a	u	t	g	a	l	l	e	y
b	e	a	m	z	b	d	y	e
f	m	k	s	i	h	p	r	f
o	o	s	t	e	r	n	i	a
r	z	y	e	c	d	g	d	g
w	c	a	m	i	g	f	i	r
a	m	i	d	s	h	i	p	s
r	b	r	i	d	g	e	s	r
d	i	s	c	o	n	n	e	c

1. kitchen on a ship: _____

2. the extreme width of a vessel: _____

3. the back end of a ship: _____

4. the midships part of a ship: _____

5. the fore end of the ship: _____

6. the bow of the ship: _____

7. where the ship's wheel is: _____

Unit 6 — What is the safety equipment for?

Part One: Safety Equipment

Conversation 1 : Where are the life rafts?

Scenario: Jack is explaining some marine safety equipment to Keiko.

davit and life rafts

Pre-Listening Questions:

1. What is Jack pointing at?
2. What is inside of the containers?

Conversation 1 : 🎧 Track 36

Keiko:	Jack, I had a horrible nightmare about our ship sinking!
Jack:	Don't worry Keiko; this is a very safe ship. In the unlikely event of

an emergency, we have enough life rafts to accommodate all people aboard.

Keiko:	Speaking of life rafts, where are they?
Jack:	Look there, in those white cylindrical containers. They are placed both on the port side amidships and the starboard side amidships.
Keiko:	In those white barrel-like things? No way.
Jack:	Yes, that's exactly where they're. The hard container is to protect the inflatable life rafts from the rain and sun. They're the latest model for long distance cruising, designed for open ocean navigation and the most challenging conditions.
Keiko:	Wow, I wonder how one uses it.
Jack:	It's pretty easy. In an emergency, we open up the white container and press the auto inflate button on the life raft. It should inflate in less than a minute. Most life rafts are equipped with nitrogen or carbon dioxide canisters. So our life rafts will inflate at the touch of a button.
Keiko:	How do rescue teams locate the life rafts in distress or a man overboard?
Jack:	Various devices can assist, for example, a marine Emergency Position Indicating Radio Beacon (EPIRB), and Search and Rescue Transponders (SARTs). They can be detected by radars carried by most vessels. Another one is Personal Locator Beacon. It has a clip attached to the lifejacket worn by individuals. With inbuilt high precision GPS receiver, fellow crew members can quickly and efficiently locate and retrieve a missing crew member.
Keiko:	Wow, these devices can greatly increase the chances of a safe rescue. Thanks, I feel safer already!
Jack:	These search and rescue locating devices are must-have devices for all people aboard.

Comprehension Questions : 🎧 Track 37

1. Where are the life rafts?
2. Why are life rafts put in the barrels?
3. Where can we find the life rafts on this ship?
4. What is a marine Emergency Position Indicating Radio Beacon for?

Conversation 2 : What is accepted as marine life-saving equipment? 🎧 Track 38

Scenario: Keiko is interested in identifying items of life-saving equipment.

Keiko: It's good to notice there're so many fire extinguishers aboard, almost one fire extinguisher located at the exit to each cabin.

Jack: The fire extinguishers in the corridors are CO_2 and dry powder type. There are portable fire extinguishers in the life boats too. Many safety guidelines also recommend a fixed automatic fire extinguisher installed in an enclosed engine space, and one larger general purpose fire extinguisher mounted in the main cabin or saloon area.

Keiko: In addition to fire extinguishers, what other life-saving equipment does a vessel carry?

Jack: Well, life jackets, life rafts, distress flares, EPIRBs, First Aid, lifebuoys, man overboard equipment, VHF Radios, radar reflectors, anchors, anchor windlass & much more.

Keiko: Is every vessel required to carry all of them?

Jack: Requirements vary based on the type of vessel you are operating, the waterway you are operating on and in some cases, your proximity to the shore.

Keiko: I know a lifebuoy ring is used for keeping a person afloat in water. But what are distress flares for?

Jack: Flares signal that you are in trouble and provide an exact location for searching vessels. The use of them indicates that there is grave and imminent danger to life or a vessel.

Keiko: These sound really cool! I guess the care of the equipment is also very important.

Jack: Right. It has been proven many times in emergency situations that quality, well maintained safety equipment saves lives.

Keiko: I see. That's why they're often kept in an accessible, sealed, waterproof container.

Jack: Yes. Advanced technologies help a lot to promote their quality. Safety equipment is generally durable and long lasting. It won't rot or mould and is unaffected by extreme weather or prolonged outdoor exposure.

Lifebuoys are all over the ship.

Comprehension Questions : 🎧 **Track 39**

1. Where on this ship can people find fire extinguishers?
2. How does a vessel decide to carry items of life-saving equipment?
3. hen do people use distress flares?
4. Where are the items of life-saving equipment often stored in order to be protected from saltwater?

Pronunciation: 🎧 **Track 40**

<table>
<tr><th colspan="3">Vowels</th></tr>
<tr><th>[æ]</th><th>[ɛ]</th><th>[e]</th></tr>
<tr><td>nap</td><td>press</td><td>safe</td></tr>
<tr><td>have</td><td>protect</td><td>inflate</td></tr>
<tr><td>satellite</td><td>electronic</td><td>container</td></tr>
<tr><td>raft</td><td>distress</td><td>place</td></tr>
<tr><td>barrel</td><td>excellent</td><td>locate</td></tr>
<tr><td>challenging</td><td>already</td><td></td></tr>
<tr><td>lifejacket</td><td>rescue</td><td></td></tr>
</table>

Part Two: Grammar, Language, Cultural Tips

A. On-Board Safety Communication 🎧 **Track 41**

＊This is your Captain speaking. We have a collision abreast the number three hatch on the port side. Water is flooding in the number three hatch. Damage control teams are fighting the flooding. The flooding is not under control yet. For safety reasons, take your lifejackets with you. I request all crew members to go to your assembly stations.

✳ Check the launching track of No 1 lifeboat and report.

The launching track of No. 1 lifeboat will be clear in 3 minutes.

Check the fuel of the lifeboat engines and report.

The fuel tank of No. 1 lifeboat engine is full.

Operate the lifeboat engines and report.

All lifeboat engines are operational.

B. Preposition of place

✳ The stevedores on the quay are ready to load the ship.

✳ The ship is moored to the quay by a number of ropes.

✳ The deckhands are working on deck.

✳ Load the cargo into the holds.

✳ The ship is at sea.

✳ The ship is on the open sea.

✳ The ship is on course (or off course).

✳ The ship is heading towards the island.

✳ The ship is in the fairway.

✳ Proceed along the fairway.

✳ The captain should remain on the bridge as much as possible during any emergency.

✳ Watchkeepers remain at stations until further order.

✳ Assemble on the foredeck.

✳ Replace the life raft container in the next port.

✳ Report the total number of persons in lifeboat.

✳ Keep lookout for persons in water.

✳ There are no dangerous targets on the radar.

✳ Lower No. 1 lifeboat alongside the embarkation deck.

✳ Jump onto the life raft alongside the vessel.

C. Emergency Report and Commands 🎧 Track 42

Report

✱ Fire is not under control.

✱ Fire spreading to dangerous goods.

✱ Oil escaping into sea.

✱ We have flooding in No. 4 hold.

✱ Man overboard on starboard side.

✱ Burnt smell from ventilators.

Commands

✱ Pick up injuries.

✱ Drop lifebuoys.

✱ Water on.

✱ Run out fire hoses.

✱ Free the blocked water pipes.

✱ Evacuate all rooms.

✱ Provide first aid.

✱ Increase pressure in the water pipes.

✱ Switch off ventilators.

✱ Clear the fire dampers（防火閥）.

✱ Shut down auxiliary engines.

D. Grammar: Gerunds and Infinitives

A gerund is the –ing form of a verb used as a noun.

1. <u>Gerunds</u> are used as the objects of certain verbs.

    Examples: We **finished eating** at 7:00.

    I **like swimming**.

    John **enjoys listening** to music.

    Would you **mind opening** the window?

    It **started raining** yesterday.

2. Gerunds are used as the objects of prepositions.

Examples: We **talked about going** to Hawaii for our vacation.

Second officer is **in charge of checking** the functioning of all electrical and monitoring system.

I **am interested in learning** more about your work.

An infinitive consists of to + the simple form of a verb.

Examples: I **hope to see** you again soon.

The teacher **wanted** the students **to finish** the assignment.

He **asked** the waitress **to get** a Coffee for him.

We **decided** not **to go** shopping.

She **promised to be** here by ten.

I **like to swim**.

It **started to rain** yesterday.

It's your turn:

1. The captain enjoy (read) _____ .
2. John is excited about (leave) _____ for New York.
3. Joe has given up (smoke) _____ .
4. I don't want (be) _____ late for the class.
5. She started (cry) _____ .

E. Ways to Tell the Function of Equipment

1. A food disposer is <u>used to grind</u> unwanted food and leftover.
2. A windlass <u>is used for moving</u> heavy objects.
3. A crane <u>is to lift</u> heavy objects.
4. We <u>lift</u> heavy objects <u>with</u> a crane.
5. The marine magnetic compass <u>is mainly used for</u> steering a course.
6. A lifebuoy ring <u>is for</u> keeping a person afloat in water.
7. A davit <u>is used to lower</u> an emergency lifeboat to the embarkation level to be boarded.

Part Three: Reading

Fire Fighting Equipment

Fighting fires on board is a challenging and difficult task. Effective fire fighting depends on good training and quality equipment. Before leaving a port, every ship must make sure that all fire fighting equipment is available and in full working order. Various types of fire might break out at any places aboard and should be put out with different types of fire extinguishers or fixed fire systems. Most often fires occur in enclosed spaces, for example, ship's engine rooms where fuel, lubricating oil, and hydraulic fluid are very close to heat sources. There are advanced devices for circumstances where a crew member suspects the beginning of a fire often signified by smoke or a burnt smell. If a fire breaks out, it must be confined first and then extinguished. It is important to remember not to use a water extinguisher on grease fires or electrical fires. The flames will spread and make the fire bigger. Water extinguishers can be used to fight the fire if you're certain it contains ordinary combustible materials only. Dry chemical extinguishers are filled with foam or powder to put out fires with flammable or combustible liquids, including petrol, grease and oil. CO_2 extinguishers can be used on electrical fires. It is vital to know what type of extinguisher to use in different fire situations. Using the wrong type of extinguisher for the wrong type of fire can be life-threatening. Sometimes, using a breathing apparatus (BA) is also a must in a complicated fire. Fire fighters may also need to put on personal protective equipment (PPE) like smoke helmets, protective clothing, and gloves to suppress the fire and get things under control. All these emergency devices need to be found nearby in case a fire.

Reading comprehension: Answer the following questions.

1. What are the two main factors to effective fire fighting?
2. Where does a fire likely break out?
3. What must be done first when a fire breaks out?

4. What type of extinguisher do we often use to extinguish electrical fires?

5. In addition to fire extinguishers, what other equipment is often used by fire fighters?

Part Four: Exercises

A. Name the safety equipment and tell when to use it.

(1)   (2)   (3)

B. Listen to the recording and guessing what safety equipment it is.
🎧 **Track 43**

C. Listen to the recording of introducing the General Emergency Alarm on a passenger ship and answer the questions.
🎧 **Track 44**

1. What does the General Emergency Alarm sound like?

2. What should passengers do when they hear the signal?

3. Where is the Muster Station on this ship?

4. What can help the passengers find the directions of going to the Must Station?

D. Match the following emergency reports and suitable commands.

Emergency report	Suitable command
( ) 1. Man overboard on starboard side.	A. Provide first aid.
( ) 2. Fire in engine room.	B. All crew assist to remove the spill.
( ) 3. Oil escaping into sea.	C. Operate the lifeboat engines.
( ) 4. Two persons injured.	D. Put out the fire.
	E. Evacuate all rooms.
	F. Drop lifebuoys.

E. Say in English.

1. 我們有足夠的救生艇可以容納所有人。

_____

2. 硬容器是保護救生艇免於日曬和雨淋。

_____

3. 它們是為長期航行而出的最新型。

_____

4. 救援隊如何找到落水人員的位置？

_____

5. 有了內建的 GPS 接收器，我們可以又快又有效率尋回失蹤的船員。

_____

6. 安全設備通常是耐用、持久的。

_____

Is it safe at sea?

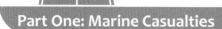

Part One: Marine Casualties

Conversation 1 An Accident at Sea

Scenario: Jack and Keiko are listening to a piece of news report about a marine casualty.

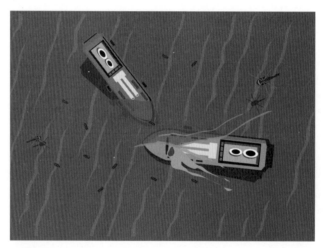

Pre-Listening Questions:

1. What case is the news about?

2. What should seafarers try their best to do when an accident happene

Conversation 1 : 🎧 Track 45

Jack:	Keiko, listen to the news report.
News report:	Excessive speed in thick fog was the main reason behind the loss of South Korean cargo ship and the death of her 16 crew members. The inquiry has largely blamed the Chinese-owned containership

Jin Sheng for causing the collision with the Golden Rose built in 1982. The two ships collided in an early, May morning some 40miles off Dalian…

Keiko: Did the tragedy happen all because of the bad weather conditions?

Jack: No, there was also human error involved.

Keiko: What do you mean by "human error"?

Jack: Well, at sea, human error could be incorrect decisions, improperly performed actions, or improper lack of actions.

Keiko: I see. In this case, both ships were traveling too fast in poor weather conditions.

Jack: Right. Besides, Golden Rose should have yielded the waterway according to the regulations.

Keiko: What else was Jin Sheng accused of?

Jack: She was accused of not reporting promptly.

Keiko: Apparently, some human errors were made in this collision case. The collision could have been prevented.

Jack: That's why seafarers need to be well trained, so they can do the right thing at the right time in response to normal and emergency situations. They should prevent loss of life and limit damage as much as possible.

Keiko: Point taken.

Comprehension Questions : 🎧 Track 46

1. How many seafarers died in this event?
2. What type of ship was Jin Sheng?
3. When was Golden Rose built?
4. Where did it happen?
5. Why do seafarers need to be well trained to respond in an emergency?

Conversation 2 : The Titanic Case 🎧 Track 47

Scenario: Kei and Jack are discussing a famous marine causality in the history.

Keiko: Was the ship Titanic very large?

Jack: It was the largest ocean liner built in its day, measuring 882 feet 9 inches long and 92 feet 6 inches at the beam.

Keiko: Why does the story of the Titanic fascinate so many people?

Jack: Well, it was considered by many as a technical marvel by its contemporaries. It had 16 watertight compartments in a 1/6-mile-long hull.

Keiko: That's why it was called an "unsinkable" vessel, right?

Jack: Yeh, but it sank on its maiden voyage just four and a half days later. More than 1,500 passengers died. Only 713 were rescued.

Keiko: Did they send out distress signals?

Jack: Yes, they did. But the ship disappeared into the bone-chilling water quickly. Besides, there were not enough lifeboats aboard.

Keiko: Did this tragedy have any impact on maritime safety?

Jack: Yes, some major changes in maritime regulations were made to implement new safety measures. For example, more lifeboats were provided aboard, the International Convention for the safety of Life at Sea (SOLAS) was established in 1914, and an International Ice Patrol was set up later. These still govern maritime safety today.

Keiko: What patrol?

Jack: International Ice Patrol. It's a twenty-four hour radio watch to monitor the presence of icebergs in the North Atlantic.

Comprehension Questions : 🎧 Track 48

1. What type of vessel was the Titanic?
2. How long was the ship?
3. Why was the Titanic called "the unsinkable vessel"?
4. How many people died in this casualty?
5. What changes were made after the tragedy?

Pronunciation 🎧 Track 49

/I/	/i/	/aI/
ship	speed	life
limit	need	mile
thick	mean	collide
simply	reason	behind
inquiry	sea	right
improper		
incorrect		
decision		
collision		
condition		

Part Two: Grammar, Cultural and Language Tips

A. Background of Standard Marine Communication Phrases (SMCP) Of IMO (International Maritime Organization, United Nations)

Professor Peter Trenkner is the principal author of IMO SMCP. According to his understanding, investigations into the human factor regarding disasters at sea revealed that one third of accidents happened primarily due to insufficient command of Maritime English. This eventually made IMO put great emphasis on how to minimize Maritime English communication problems. As a result, IMO adopted the Standard Marine Communication Phrases in 2001. Therefore, the SMCP have been available since 2001 for communicating effectively by using standard phrases in preference to other wordings in all essential safety-related situations. (information from *Alert*, Issue No. 14, May 2007)

According to IMO, SMCP "was drafted intentionally in a simplified version of Maritime English to reduce grammatical, lexical and idiomatic varieties to a tolerable minimum, using standardized structures for the sake of its function aspects.(IMO)" (see examples in B and C)

B. Omission of Function Words in the SMCP

1. Omission of articles

   Where is the fire? ~~The~~ Fire is in deck.

   Pick up ~~the~~ injuries.

   Report ~~the~~ damage.

   Send ~~a~~ helicopter with ~~a~~ doctor.

2. Omission of verb be

   Is smoke toxic? No, smoke ~~is~~ not toxic.

   No person ~~is~~ injured.

   Fire ~~is~~ not under control.

   Fire ~~is~~ spreading to the engine room.

Hatch covers ~~are~~ in order.

Hold ventilation system ~~is~~ operational.

3. Omission of the auxiliary "have"

　Has vessel refloated? No, vessel ~~has~~ not refloated.

4. Omission of Subject and verb be

　~~I am~~ Ready for the helicopter.

5. Omission of "there be"

　Are there dangers to navigation? ~~There are~~ No danger to navigation.

C. Describing Marine Incidents and Accidents

An incident is something that happens and it could lead to an accident and needs to be reported. An accident is when something bad happens with no intention to cause harm to the safety of a ship, an individual or the environment. Marine accidents may be classified according to different levels of casualties, like a death of or injury to people, the loss of a ship, material damage to a ship, severe damage to the environment, etc.

1. A close quarters situation:

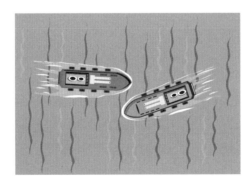

(a) Two vessels pass in close proximity of each other with a high risk of collision;

(b) One vessel passes so close to an object that there was a risk of collision by the vessel with the object.

close quarters (n.): a situation of being uncomfortably close to someone or something

* This is a close quarters situation! The two vessels might <u>collide with</u>/<u>run into</u> each other.

2. A collision:

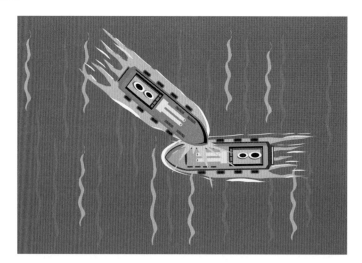

Marine collision can occur between two vessels or a ship and a floating structure like an offshore drilling platform or an ice berg or even a port, resulting in a damaging accident.

＊Two vessels collided with each other off the coast of Keelung.

＊A ship ran into a reef off the coast of Shanghai, China, tearing a big hole in the hull, and sank 5 hours later.

When a ship collision occurs, it may result in immeasurable consequences. For example, the loss of life is always an irreparable damage and something that can never be compensated for. It may bring the environmental impact which is very negative especially if the vessels in the collision happen to carry any chemicals or any other harmful material that could be dangerous for marine life.

3. Grounding

A ship grounding occurs when a ship runs aground and makes contact with the bed of the sea. The dangers caused by a ship grounding vary according to the vessel and the situation that lead to the impact. If the vessel is stranded on the bed that it contacts, this may create a difficult process to free it. The grounding may also allow water to flood the lower part of the ship or cause oil spills. Ships can sink as a result of a ship grounding. Very similar to the consequences of a ship collision, ships carrying dangerous cargo may harm the environment if they run aground.

4. Fire on board

Fire on board is one of the most serious risks for property and persons, as well as for the surrounding environment. On board there are tons of liquid fuel, electrical equipment, air-conditioning plants, engines, boilers, and flammable material, not to mention a high percentage of solid and liquid goods that are flammable or at least combustible in cargo ships.

D. Safety Problems at Sea & Incident Report

Marine casualties may be caused by the following problems.

＊ loss of main propulsion
＊ loss of generator power
＊ loss of steering
＊ fire/explosion
＊ flooding
＊ grounding
＊ collision
＊ sinking
＊ person overboard
＊ spill/cargo spill
＊ overflow
＊ leaking
＊ list
＊ armed attack/piracy

Incident Report

＊ Where is the fire?
Fire is in hold No. 4.
Are dangerous goods on fire?
No, dangerous goods are not on fire.
Is the fire under control?
No, fire is not under control. REQUEST. I require fire fighting assistance.

＊ I am flooding in the engine room. I cannot control flooding. REQUEST. I require pumps.
I will send pumps.

＊ Have you been in collision? I have collided with unknown object.
Have you received any damage in collision? I have received serious damage to bottm plate. I am in danger of list to port side. REQUEST I require tug assistance.
I am proceeding to your assistance.

＊ What part of your vessel is aground? Aground forward.
What damage have you received?   I have minor damage.

＊ The ship was under attack by pirates. Two men injured. I have some damage to navigational equipment.
Can you proceed?
I can only proceed at slow speed.
WARNING. Rocks in position 38° North of the fairway are uncharted.
What kind of assistance is required?
I require medical assistance and tug assistance.

E. Distress Message Format 🎧 Track 50

* A Mayday distress call can be sent only when a ship is in grave and imminent danger which threatens life and immediate assistance is required. The message should be spoken slowly and clearly in a particular format as follows.

MAYDAY MAYDAY MAYDAY
This is MV Blue Highway, MV Blue Highway, MV Blue Highway. (three times of vessel name)
MAYDAY, MV Blue Highway, Call sign Quebec 5 Whisky Yankee, MMSI 123456789.
Position 35°12'0" N and 102°10'0"E at 1340 UTC (position)
I am on fire in the cargo tanks and have dangerous list to starboard. (nature of distress)
I require fire pumps and medical assistance. (nature of assistance)
Six persons on board and two injured badly. (number of persons aboard and condition of any injured)
We have some damage to navigational equipment. (seaworthiness of the vessel)
The color of my hull is dark blue, over. (description of the vessel)

* A Pan-Pan urgency call is sent when safety of a person or vessel is in jeopardy, but the danger is not life threatening. Transmission of a Pan-Pan also follows the same format as the May Day message.

PAN PAN, PAN PAN, PAN PAN
This is MV Blue Highway, MV Blue Highway, MV Blue Highway.
PAN PAN, MV Blue Highway, Call sign Quebec 5 Whisky Yankee, MMSI 12345678.
I am flooding in the engine room.
I require pumps.
Five persons on board, no one injured.
Flooding is not under control. We are presently trying to pump out excess water, over.

F. Adverbs

1. Adverbs modify verbs.

   The inquiry has **largely** <u>blamed</u> the Chinese-owned containership Jin Sheng

   Was the tragedy **simply** <u>caused</u> by bad weather conditions?

2. Adverbs modify adjectives.

   Human errors could be incorrect decisions, **improperly** <u>performed</u> actions, or improper lack of actions.

3. Adverbs modify adverbs.

   Both ships were traveling **too** <u>fast</u> in poor weather conditions.

Part Three: Reading

Responding to Emergencies

Major emergencies at sea are in fact, very rare in the world. When an emergency does occur, those onboard will be under extreme duress. The situation needs to be assessed accurately and decisions need to be executed precisely. Mistakes can be life-threatening. The only way the ship's personnel can prepare themselves is through endless training.

In any crisis, the first and foremost aim is to ensure that cries for help can be heard. Maritime distress signals are laid down and defined by the "International Regulation for Preventing Collisions at Sea" and the "International Code of Signals". A Mayday distress call can be sent only when there are grave, life-threatening dangers. Any other urgent messages not involving in life-

threatening should be sent via a Pan-Pan message. The most commonly used way of sending distress signals out is by radio or tapping out SOS in Morse code. Other methods include using red flares, or canister that emits colored smoke. Furthermore guns or other explosive signals should be fired once per minute. At whatever cost, pleas for help must be heard as soon as possible.

To assist personnel in responding to emergencies, many operators and ship owners have an emergency response plan, sometimes called a "contingency plan". It is relatively unusual for new types of accidents to occur on board and many of those that continue to occur are due to unsafe acts by seafarers. The challenge for trainers and training, and managers ashore and afloat, is how to minimize these unsafe acts. This involves not only the professional skills but also the attitudes necessary to ensure safety objectives are met. In the plan, seafarers will recognize that accidents are preventable through correct procedures and established best practice; they will also be asked to constantly thinking safety and seeking continuous improvement.

Circle T for True or F for False for Each of the Following Statements

1. Major emergencies at sea are in fact very rare in the world.   T / F
2. Ship's personnel need to be prepared through endless training to make good decisions in an emergency.   T / F
3. When an emergency happens, the first and foremost aim is to abandon the ship.   T / F
4. Never fire guns or other explosive signals because it is very dangerous.   T / F
5. There is only one way to send out distress signals.   T / F

Answer the Following Questions

1. How will ship's personnel feel when an emergency occur?
2. What may happen if an emergency situation is not assessed accurately and big mistakes are made?
3. What is the first and foremost aim in any crisis?
4. What is a contingency plan?
5. What does a contingency aim at?

Part Four: Exercises

A. Identify the Incident by Choosing One from the List Based on What You Hear.

Case A 🎧 **Track 51**

☐Oil Spill ☐Grounding ☐Fire ☐Collision

Case B 🎧 **Track 52**

☐Oil Spill ☐Grounding ☐Fire ☐Collision

B. Say and Write in English

1. Victory 號擱淺了。

_____

2. 船的哪部分擱淺？

_____

3. 船中央擱淺了。

_____

4. Victory 號右側傾斜嚴重。

_____

5. 擱淺後 Victory 現在在下沉。

_____

6. 這個碰撞原本可以避免的。

_____

7. 他們有送出遇險信號嗎？

_____

8. Titanic 在處女航就沉了。

_____

C. Fill in the blank.

✱ A: I am _____ attack by pirates. Two men injured. I have some damage to navigational equipment.

B: Can you proceed?

A: I can only proceed at slow _____ .

B: _____ . Uncharted rocks are ahead. What kind of _____ is required?

A: _____ I require medical assistance and tug assistance.

D. Pair work

Choose either one of the following cases and decide what kind of distress call you and your partner need to send. You may need to create information you need for the distress call. Then present the messages in class.

Case A

At 1720 UTC, fishing vessel *Flying Fox* is some miles west of the Bahamas. The ship suffered an engine failure and the captain ordered the ship to divert and look for the best anchorage so that the engine could be repaired. Suddenly, the ship grounded. They expect to refloat when tide rises with tug assistance.

Case B

The "Morning Star" ferry is sailing with 22 crew members and 90 passengers on board. The captain received a fire report in the accommodating spaces. The fire was quickly extinguished but shortly afterwards a second fire broke out in the after part of the gangway. The fire spread rapidly and 3 crew members were injured. The captain ordered evacuation and abandon the vessel, considering that the fire could no longer be controlled. All passengers have sat down in the lifeboats.

E. Surf on the Internet to find a ship collision case and report in class. Then the whole class discusses the consequences.

I request urgent medical advice.

Part One: Medical Emergencies

Conversation 1 : Open the airway

Scenario: Jack is taking a first aid training course. The trainer is showing how to help keep the unresponsive person safe and prevent further harm.

CALL EMERGENCY NUMBER

CHECK BREATHING

LIFT CHIN CHECK BREATHING

GIVE RESCUE BREATHS

PERFORM CPR

Pre-listening Questions:

1. What is the case they talk about to deal with?
2. What do Jack need to do if the casualty does not have normal breathing?

Conversation 1 : 🎧 Track 53

Trainer:	If someone is unresponsive and breathing, the first thing is to keep their airway open so they can still breathe.
Jack:	What if the person' mouth does not open?
Trainer:	Place one hand on the casualty's forehead and gently tilt the person's head back. As you do this, the mouth will fall open slightly. Then place the fingertips of your other hand on the point of the person's chin and lift the chin.

Jack:	Can we always do this to the casualty who has other injury?
Trainer:	Not always. If you think the person could have a spinal injury, you must keep the person's neck as still as possible, instead of tilting the neck.
Jack:	How do I do that?
Trainer:	Place your hands on either side of their face and with your fingertips gently lift the jaw to open the airway, avoiding any movement of their neck.
Jack:	Ok. If I keep checking the person's breathing, and found weak breaths, should I start CPR immediately?
Trainer:	Yes. Repeat 30 times, at a rate of about twice a second until the medical help comes. Unresponsiveness can last for a few seconds or for a long time.
Jack:	What are the common causes resulting in the unresponsiveness?
Trainer:	Well, it's often brought on by serious illness or injury, or by taking alcohol or other drugs. If you can collect some information and report to the medical team, that helps.

Comprehension Questions : 🎧 Track 54

1. What is the first thing to do with an unresponsive breathing person?
2. Why do the first aiders tilt the casualty's head back and lift his or her chin?
3. What should the first aiders do with the casualty's neck if the person has a spinal injury?
4. When do the first aiders start CPR?
5. What are the most possible reasons which cause the unresponsiveness?

Conversation 2 : Is the pain central or all over your abdomen?
🎧 Track 55

Scenario: A cadet has a sudden sharp colic. Captain is asking him some questions to deal with the problem.

Captain:	Is the pain central or all over your abdomen? I am going to lay my hand on your abdomen. Tell me where you feel the most severe pain, ok?
Cadet:	Ok. Ouch!
Captain:	It seems to be on the right side of your abdomen. When did it start?
Cadet:	I felt a continuous and severe pain starting about an hour ago.
Captain:	What other symptoms do you have, combined with pain in the abdomen, vomiting or diarrhea?
Cade:	I have nausea.

Captain:	Let me take your temperature and measure your pulse rate. Have you had chills?
Cade:	Yes, a little bit.
Captain:	Your temperature is normal at present. Pulse rate is rapid. I will have them keep a record of the temperatures and pulse rates every 2 hours. Did you have problems of gallstones or appendicitis before?
Cade:	No, Sir.
Captain:	I 'll need to observe for a couple of hours and see how it goes. After I make an accurate diagnosis, then treatment should be described to you.
Cade:	Thank you, Sir.

Comprehension Questions : 🎧 Track 56

1. Why does the captain lay his hand on the cadet's abdomen?
2. What other symptoms does the cadet have associated with abdominal pain?
3. What information will the captain put in the record?
4. When will the captain give treatment to the cadet?

Pronunciation : Word Stress 🎧 Track 57

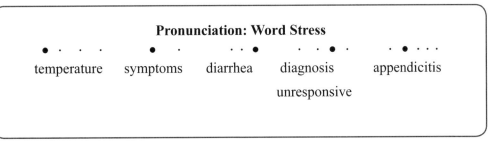

Pronunciation: Word Stress

temperature   symptoms   diarrhea   diagnosis   appendicitis

unresponsive

Part Two: Grammar, Cultural and Language Tips

A. Common types of diseases and injuries at sea

Diseases	Possible symptoms
cold	have a fever/headache/a sore throat/ a runny nose/a frequent cough/yellow sputum/nausea feel dizzy blow one's nose sneeze be all stuffed up vomit
ulcer of stomach	have severe and continuous pain, worst in the upper part of the abdomen have heartburn
food allergy	have itching in the mouth have hives, itching or eczema have swelling of the lips, face, tongue and throat or other parts of the body have wheezing, nasal congestion or trouble breathing have abdominal pain, diarrhea, nausea or vomiting have dizziness, lightheadedness or fainting
asthma	have coughing especially at night have wheezing have shortness of breath feel chest tightness, pain, or pressure

Diseases or injuries	Causes
appendicitis	The inflammation caused by the appendix may burst into the abdominal cavity giving rise to peritonitis.
burns	A burn is caused by dry heat, e.g., flame, friction, sunburn, acid, or electric current.
scalds	A scald is caused by moist heat, e.g., steam or boiling liquid.

intestinal colic	It is due to over-action of the muscles of the intestines because of some indigestible matter.
renal colic	Stones form in the kidneys.
dislocations	A dislocation of a joint occurs because of the extreme normal mobility of the joint.
heatstroke or heat exhaustion	This occurs with the effects of unusually environmental heat on the human body.
paralysis	This is due to loss of muscular power caused by some disease or injury of the nervous system.

B. Expressions of medical dialogues 🎧 **Track 58**

✳ **Examples of describing physical symptoms:**

-What seems to be the problem?	My throat is sore and I have a fever.
-What's the matter?	My arm hurts. Swelling is hot and red. Pain is increased by hand pressure.
-How do you feel?	I feel tired and awful. Temperature is rising.
-Do you have a stomachache?	No, but I have a backache. Pain is a dull ache.
-Have you have headaches?	Yes, pain radiates to my ears. I also have felt dizzy.
-Is bleeding severe?	Bleeding is not severe.

✳ **Giving medical instructions or advice.** 🎧 **Track 59**

-I want to check you lungs. Breathe in. Breathe out. Cough.

-Apply ice-cold compress and renew every 4 hours.

-Put patient to bed lying down at absolute rest.

-Give no solid food of any kind.

-Sips of water only by mouth.

-Record pulse rate every 2 hours, temperature every 6 hours.

-Seek medical advice by radio.

-You should give aspirin tablets.

C. Check if you understand the common items of Marine First-Aid Kit

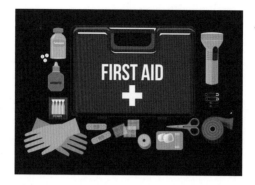

- Sun block
- Insect repellant
- Anti-itch lotion or cream for treating insect bites, sunburn, and skin irritations
- Adhesive bandages in assorted sizes
- narrow adhesive strips, for gaping cuts
- Individually wrapped, sterile gauze pads (2" and 4") to control bleeding
- Hypoallergenic adhesive tape to hold a dressing or splint in place
- Roll of absorbent cotton, as padding for a splint
- Sterile roller bandages (2" and 3"), at least 3 rolls, to support sprained muscles
- Cotton-tipped swabs
- Eye drops
- Thermometer
- Antiseptic ointment, spray, or towel for cleansing wounds
- Antibiotic ointment to prevent infection of minor wounds
- Bottled water to rinse wounds
- Clean towels or compress, to control bleeding or as a wrap for ice
- Chemical ice packs
- First Aid handbook

＊Pair work. Take turns naming 3 items and explaining the purposes for using them.

D. Read medical case description. This is given when request for medical assistance.

I have a male aged <u>34</u> years. Patient has been ill for <u>3</u> days. Patient has suffered from <u>acute pain in the region of the bladder</u>. Onset was <u>gradual</u>. Patient has been given <u>penicillin injection in last 40 hours</u> without effect. General condition of the patient has worsened. Patient has fits of shivering. Temperature taken in mouth is 40. Pulse rate per minute is 110. The rate of breathing per minute is 22. Patient has severe cough too. Patient has yellow sputum. My probable diagnosis is Cystitis combined with pneumonia.

Questions:

1. Which word has the same meaning of "onset"?

   situation   beginning   pain   course

2. What does the phrase "fits of shivering" mean?

   unconscious   a state of shock   chills   hot and dry

3. What does "onset was gradual" refer to?

4. What general symptoms does the patient have?

E. What request do you make for medical assistance? (SMCP)

A: I require medical assistance. I have a male aged 45 years. Patient has head injury. Pulse rate per minute is 95. Pulse is weak. Vomiting is absent.

B: Do you have doctor on board?

A: No, I have no doctor on board.

B: What kind of assistance is required?

A: I require helicopter with doctor to pick up person.

(Other kinds of medical assistance could be boat for hospital transfer or radio medical advice.)

Part Three: Reading

Ships are typically semi closed with crowded living accommodation, shared sanitary facilities and common food and water supplies. Such conditions could facilitate the spread of infectious diseases. The majority of general cargo vessels have no medical personnel onboard. Passengers and crew could be at greater risk than people onshore if health care facilities onboard are limited.

The health and economic consequences of some diseases can be serious. Death may occur just within a few hours. A search regarding diseases showed that the most frequent events on board are the outbreaks of food and waterborne diseases. Factors contributing to the food borne outbreaks included deficiencies in food hygiene and infected food handlers. Factors contributing to the waterborne outbreaks included cross connections between drinkable and non-drinkable water, improper loading procedures, poor design and construction of drinkable water storage tanks and inadequate disinfection.

The World Health Organization published a *Guide to Ship Sanitation* standardizing the sanitary measures taken in ships, to safeguard the health of travelers and to prevent the spread of infection from one country to another. It covers the issues of drinkable water supply, drinkable water system on board ships, swimming pool safety, waste disposal, food safety and vermin control.

Discussion questions:

1. In what ways do ship conditions facilitate the spread of infectious diseases?
2. What may be the consequences of some diseases occurring on ship?

Part Four: More Exercises

A. Say and Write in English to describe physical symptoms.

1. 我的腳受傷了。

2. 病人的呼吸微弱。

_____

3. 體溫正上升中。

_____

4. 她的右手部燒傷。

_____

5. 他的胃有灼熱感。

_____

6. 流血嚴重嗎？

_____

7. 他每分鐘的脈搏是 80 下。

_____

B. Listening Task: Common injuries seafarers must be aware of
🎧 Track 60

Comprehension questions:

1. What is the purpose of this talk?
2. What are the very common personal injuries mentioned in this talk?
3. Why do some accidents occur to seafarers and hurt their hands even though they do wear gloves to protect hands?
4. How do seafarers do to prevent head injuries?

C. Listening Task: requesting medical assistance. 🎧 Track 61

Comprehension Questions:

1. How long has the patient been ill?
2. Where is the pain?
3. Is the patient vomiting?
4. What is the probable diagnosis?
5. What kind of assistance will the ship get?

How's the weather?

Part One: Weather Forecast

Conversation 1 : Shipping Forecast

Scenario: Keiko is learning to understand a BBC Shipping Forecast.

Pre-listening Questions:

1. Identify the locations of the sea areas when you are listening.
2. When is the shipping forecast issued?
3. What will be the weather like?

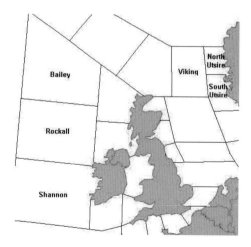

Forecast:

Conversation 1 : 🎧 **Track 62**

BBC Shipping Forecast:	The Shipping Forecast issued by the Met Office. On behalf of the Maritime and Coastguard Agency, at 1725 on Saturday 07 July 2012. There are warnings of gales in Shannon Rockall and Bailey. The general synopsis at 1500 low just west of Shannon 987 expected Bailey 983 by 0800 tomorrow.
Viking North Utsire South Utsireor:	Northwest 4 or 5, increasing 6 veering north 4 or 5 later, moderate, occasionally rough at first, rain or drizzle later, moderate good, occasionally poor.
Keiko:	I don't understand the terms they used. It sounds quite different from the normal weather forecast we get ashore.
Captain:	The shipping forecast uses a standard and abbreviated format to pass lots of information in a short period of time. If you know what's being said and in what order, you'll gain an understanding of the weather condition, even in poor reception areas.
Keiko:	What's being said and in what order? Please explain it again.
Captain:	First, they'll tell you time and date of the forecast. Then gale warnings issued with details of the sea areas to which they apply. The general synopsis stuff is an overview. In this case, at 1500 a low air pressure moves to the west of Shannon, with a barometric pressure of 987. A barometer is an instrument that measures air pressure. Low pressure tends to produce unsettled, poor weather. It's expected to move to Bailey with a barometric pressure of 983 by 0800 Sunday 08 July. 987 and 983 are no big difference, so it means that the conditions won't change much. Then the forecast goes to the sea areas Viking, North Utsire and South Utsire. They're located northeast of the UK.
Keiko:	What exactly is "Northwest 4 or 5, increasing 6"?
Captain:	Northwest is the direction the wind is blowing from, and the

numbers indicate the strength of the wind. Windspeed is measured as Beaufort force 4 or 5, and then increasing to force 6. But the wind will change its direction to the North in a clockwise direction. That's what veering means. After the wind report, the forecast tells the sea state. That's moderate occasionally rough at first.

Keiko: I got it. "Rain or drizzle later" is what the weather will be like.

Captain: You're right. At the end is the visibility on the sea. Visibility is generally divided into four categories: good, moderate, poor and very poor. Good means visible for greater than 5 nautical miles and moderate means greater than 2 but less than 5 nautical miles. When visibility is reduced to between 1000 meters and 2 nautical miles, we use poor. Very poor indicates visibility less than 1000 meters.

Keiko: Thank you for explaining all these to me.

(Source adapted from: Shipping Area Forecast, The UK Sea Kayak Guidebook, from http://www.ukseakayakguidebook.co.uk/understanding_forecasts/shipping_forecast.htm)

Comprehension Questions : 🎧 Track 63

1. What information in the forecast is expected to tell first?
2. Where is the wind blowing from?
3. Will the strength of the wind increase or decrease?
4. How many categories is visibility divided?
5. What does it mean when the visibility on the sea is poor?

Conversation 2 : Inshore Waters Forecast 🎧 Track 64

Scenario: Keiko and Jack are reading and discussing a text Inshore Waters Forecast.

Jack: What are you reading?

Keiko: I'm reading the inshore waters forecast. I'm figuring it out myself. The captain just taught me all about Shipping area forecast. They're quite similar.

Jack: Cool! Sounds interesting.

Keiko: OK, it came out first with time and date of the forecast, period of validity, and the area of inshore waters.

Jack: What does the forecast say about the weather?

Keiko: "Wind, westerly 3or 4 becoming variable 3, becoming northwest 4 by tomorrow morning."

Jack: Do you understand what it means?

Keiko: Well, the wind is coming from the west, windspeed force 3 or 4 but likely to vary. It'll become Northwest 4 in the area by tomorrow morning.

Jack: Good for you! Often, the wind direction changes. If the wind changes direction in a clockwise sense, it's called veering, for example, Southwest to West. And if it changes direction in a counter clockwise sense, it's called backing, like Southeast to Northeast.

Keiko: I see. The following is, "occasional rain or showers, mainly in the east."

Jack: It'll rain a bit in the East.

Keiko: Visibility is moderate or good, occasionally poor at first.

Jack: What about sea state?

Keiko: Smooth or slight, increasing moderate or rough. But I'm not sure about the differences among them, smooth, slight, moderate and rough.

Jack: Smooth refers to wave height less than 0.5 meter. Slight, wave height of slight is about 0.5 to 1.25. Moderate, 1.25 to 2.5 meters. Rough, 2.5 to 4.0.

Comprehension Questions :  Track 65

1. What information is always given first in an inshore waters forecast?
2. What does the forecast say about the wind?
3. What do people describe when the wind changes its direction from southeast to northeast?
4. What does the forecast say about visibility?
5. What will the sea state be like?

Pronunciation: Vowelss   Track 66

[e]	[I]	[aI]
rain	wind	high
sailor	visibility	right
mainly	condition	quite
gale	different	life
wave		
date		

Part Two: Grammar, Language, Cultural Tips

A. Weather Forecast on Land

* Chief Forecaster's Assessment: Track 67

London

An area of low pressure will move westwards across southern Britain from the near continent during Friday. As it does so, it will draw a plume of warm, moist air westwards across many parts of central Britain. This is likely to bring some very heavy and locally thundery rain, with totals of 20 to 40 mm quite widely and perhaps exceeding 60 or even 70 mm in these places. The public should be prepared for the possibility for surface water flooding, particularly within the Amber area, where there is an increasing likelihood of river flooding, disruption to travel and outdoor activities.

Weather of London

Headline: Occasional rain or showers. A few sunny intervals.

△ Today:

Rather cloudy with showers, and also some longer spells of rain, especially in the East at first.

A few intervals of warm sunshine are expected, but mainly during the afternoon. Maximum Temperature 22 °C.

△ Tonight:

Variable cloud with a few clear intervals and just a little rain here and there but dry for the most part, although more persistent rain may reach Hampshire later. Minimum temperature 13 °C.

△ Saturday:

Some bright or sunny intervals but also with heavy and thundery showers developing, especially by the afternoon. Maximum temperature 21 °C.

❋ **Questions based on the report:**

1. What will happen when the low pressure moves westwards from the near continent?

_____

2. What should people in Amber area do?

_____

3. What will be the temperature in London tonight?

_____

4. What will be the weather like in London Saturday?

_____

B. Terminology for Marine Forecast

＊Shipping forecast terms are defined so that forecasts are as concise as possible while being consistent with clarity. The following terms are often shown in marine forecasts around the world.

Terminology for Marine Forecast

Gale warning	Gale: Winds of at least Beaufort force 8 (34-40 knots)
	Severe gale: Winds of force 9 (41-47 knots) or gusts reaching 52-60 knots)
	Storm: Winds of force 10 (48-55 knots) or gusts reaching 61-68 knots)
	Violent storm: Winds of force 11 (56-63 knots) or gusts of 69 knots or more)
	Hurricane force: Winds of force 12 (64 knots or more))
Visibility	Very Poor: Visibility less than 1,000 metres
	Poor: Visibility between 1,000 metres and 2 nautical miles
	Moderate: Visibility between 2 and 5 nautical miles
	Good: Visibility more than 5 nautical miles
Wind	Wind direction: the direction from which the wind is blowing
	Becoming cyclonic: There will be considerable change in wind direction across the path of a depression within the forecast area.
	Veering: The changing of the wind direction clockwise, e.g. SW to W
	Backing: The changing of the wind in the opposite direction to veering (anticlockwise), e.g. SE to E
Sea State	Smooth: Wave height less than 0.5 m
	Slight: Wave height of 0.5 to 1.25 m
	Moderate: Wave height of 1.25 to 2.5 m
	Rough: Wave height of 2.5 to 4.0 m
	Very rough: Wave height of 4.0 to 6.0 m
	High: Wave height of 6.0 to 9.0 m
	Very high: Wave height of 9.0 to 14.0 m
	Phenomenal: Wave height more than 14.0 m

※ 備註：美式用法 meter 或 metre 都可；英式用法為 metre。

(information source from http://weather.mailasail.com/Franks-Weather/Marine-Weather-Forecast-Terms)

Sea Forecast	Pusan	Dalian
wind	southeast 3, increasing 4, backing east 5 later	north 5 or 6, occasionally 7
sea state	slight	rough
weather	mainly fair	rain or drizzle later
visibility	fog	moderate, occasionally very poor

Questions:

1. What is the wind speed and direction in Pusan?
2. How is the sea state in Dalian?
3. What is the weather like in Pusan?
4. How is the visibility in Dalian?

C. Marine Forecast

Bulletin issued at 09:00 HKT 14/Aug/2021

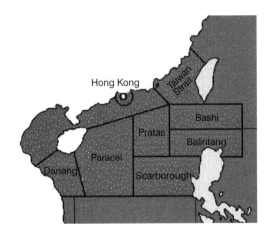

GALE WARNING AREAS: BASHI AND BALINTANG.

GENERAL SITUATION AT 130900 UTC:

THE SOUTHWESTERLY AIRSTREAM IS GENERALLY AFFECTING THE FORECAST AREAS.

MARINE FORECAST FOR 24 HOURS FROM 140100 UTC:

HONG KONG: E 3-4. ISOL SHOWERS. TEMP 32-27 C.

TAIWAN STRAIT: S TO SE 4-5, NC LATER ISOL SHOWERS. SEA 3-4 M.

BASHI: N TO NE 6-7, CYCLONIC 8 LATER. FRQ HEAVY SQUALLY SHOWERS AND TS. SEA 4-6 M. VISIBILITY 1-2 NAUTICAL MILES

SCARBOROUGH: SW 4-5, NW 5-6 SCT SQUALLY SHOWERS AND TS. SEA 2-3 M.

PRATAS: SE 4-5, N TO NE 5-6, OCNL SHOWERS.

PARACEL: S TO SW 4-5 CLD SEA UP TO 1.25 M

DANANG: SW 4-5 DZ SEA UP TO 2 M

Abbreviations may be used in the text form of marine forecasts:

ISOL = isolated

TEMP = temperature

FRQ = frequent

NC = no change

SCT = scattered

OCNL = occasional

CLD = cloudy

DZ = drizzle

TS = thunderstorm

＊The date and time are specified by a 6-digit number DDHHMM. DD stands for the day of month, HH represents the hour while MM indicates the minute in UTC.

Questions:

1. When is the forecast issued? _____

2. What areas are expected to have gale? _____

3. What is the weather like in Hong Kong? _____

4. What is the wind direction in Taiwan Strait, now and later? _____

5. How is the sea state in Bashi? _____

6. How is the visibility in Bashi? _____

7. What is the weather like in Scarborough? _____

8. What is the wind speed and direction in Danang? _____

D. Conjunctions

Conjunctions:

1. We use conjunctions like **and, but, or** to connect words or phrases that have the same grammatical functions in a sentence.

   Example: The term "rough" **and** "high" are referring to the conditions of sea surface, mainly waves.

2. A conjunction may be used to connect two independent clauses.

   Example: Good means visible for greater than 5 nautical miles **and** moderate means greater than 2 **but** less than 5 nautical miles.

   He was tired, **so** he went to bed.

   You must finish your work **before** you go home.

   When visibility is reduced to between 1000 meters and 2 nautical miles, we use poor.

   I didn't go **because** it rained hard.

   If the wind changes direction in a clockwise sense, it's called veering.

Practice: It's your turn.

   Combine the two sentences in each set.

   1. It was raining hard.

      There was a strong wind.

      _____

   2. These shoes are old.

      The shoes are comfortable.

      _____

   3. We have to hurry.

      We are late.

      _____

Part Three: Reading

Perfect Storm

The movie *Perfect Storm* is based on one of the most terrifying natural events in the twentieth century. The movie story tells how a small group of fishermen faced a powerful storm in the North Atlantic. This group of six fishermen, down on their luck, decided to go for one last run in the unpredictable and dangerous October weather in 1991. In this incidence fortune did not favor them. Warm air from a low-pressure system coming from one direction met a flow of cool and dry air generated by a high-pressure from another direction. Then the tropical Hurricane Grace joined in with the two to hit the coast of Gloucester, Massachusetts. The men in the fishing boat *Andrea Gail* were caught in a struggle with all of nature's fearsome might. They have never been found since then.

This super storm was the result of a meteorological, freak coincidence. A senior meteorologist in Boston explained how the special weather conditions combined to create a "perfect situation" to generate such a powerful storm. These combinations of events gave rise to an abnormally powerful storm with the wind speed of over 74 mph and waves over 100 feet tall. Owing to the story, the phrase "perfect storm" is coined to mean a "worst-case scenario". Although this storm was powerful, there have been other storms that have exceeded its strength. Changing weather patterns caused by global warming could make huge storms more frequent.

Answer the following questions:

1. Where did the story take place?
2. When did it happen?
3. What was the story about?
4. What happened to the crew of the *Andrea Gail*?
5. What is the connotation of the phrase "perfect storm"?

Part Four: Exercises

A. Matching the words with the descriptions.

barometer   breeze   calm   crest   downwind   foam   fronts   humid
moderate   moist   ripple   sleet   violent   visibility

_____ 1. moving air masses in the atmosphere, formed when warm air masses and cold air masses come together

_____ 2. slightly wet

_____ 3. hot and slightly wet

_____ 4. a mixture of snow and rain

_____ 5. an instrument that measures air pressure

_____ 6. a light wind

_____ 7. quiet

_____ 8. a very small wave

_____ 9. average

_____ 10. the highest part of a wave

_____ 11. how far or well you can see

_____ 12. very strong

_____ 13. small white bubbles

_____ 14. same direction as wind

B. Listen to the shipping forecast and fill in the blanks. 🎧 **Track 68**

Shipping forecast --The area forecasts for the next 24 hours:

Viking

• Gale warning issued 28 June 1527.

• _____ gale force 8 expected soon.

• South-easterly _____ 5 to 7, occasionally gale 8 at first.

• Thundery rain then _____ .

- _____ or good, occasionally poor at first.

German Bight

- Northeast 4 or 5, _____ 4 later.
- _____ later.
- Moderate or _____ .

Humber

- North 4, becoming _____ 5 or 6, then becoming _____ 4 later.
- Thundery rain then _____ , _____ at first.
- Moderate or good, occasionally _____ at first.

C. Listen to the above weather forecast again and answer the following questions. 🎧 Track 68

1. Which day is the forecast issued?
2. What will the weather be like in Viking?
3. What is the visibility?

D. Information gap.

Student A

Sea Forecast	Shanghai	Osaka
wind		north 5 or 6, occasionally 7
sea state	moderate	
weather	mainly fair	rain or drizzle later
visibility		

Student B

Sea Forecast	Shanghai	Osaka
wind	southwest 4 or 5	
sea state		slight or moderate, occasionally rough
weather		
visibility	good	moderate, occasionally poor

E. **Find a weather forecast from the newspaper and perform your weather report for the class.**

Do not overtake the vessel ahead of you.

Conversation 1 : Cargo Loading

Scenario: The container ship, MV Lalu is going to load cargo and leave the port. The Chief Officer, Jim, is now on the vessel's navigating bridge. He is in contact with the Second Officer, Scott.

A gantry crane, pictures from EVERGREEN MARINE CORP.

Pre-Listening Questions:

1. What is the Chief Officer doing?

2. What are the preparations for?

Conversation 1 : 🎧 **Track 69**

Chief Officer: Scott, this is Jim. The cargo list is complete. Have you checked the stowage plan yet?

Second Officer: Yes, the stowage plan is complete. The stability calculations are done.

Chief Officer: Good. Prepare holds and unlock the hatch covers. Report back to me when everything down in the holds is clear. We'll start loading in one hour.

(After a while the Second Officer reports back.)

Second Officer: Jim, hatch covers in order, hold lights switched on, hold ventilation system operational. The holds are clean and free of smell. The safety arrangements in the holds are operational.

Chief Officer: Instruct the crane drivers and keep within the safe working load of the cranes.

(Jim is in contact with Scott again to check the loading.)

Chief Officer: Scott, when do you expect to complete loading?

Chief Officer: Everything will be finished by 1500 hours. We're loading at 2,000 tons per hour and there're about 5,000 tons to load.

Captain: Very good. Do not exceed the loading rate of 2,000 tons per hour. The Pilot will come on board by 1600.

Comprehension Questions 🎧 **Track 70**

1. According to the information, what documents are checked before loading?
2. What does the Second Officer need to check in the holds?
3. What does the Chief Officer emphasize about loading?
4. Who will come to help the vessel leave the port?

Conversation 2 : Entering the VTS area 🎧 Track 71

Scenario: Morning Christina is contacting Vessel Traffic Service (VTS) Station of Keelung Port before arriving at the VTS zone.

Morning Christina: Keelung VTS Station, Keelung VTS Station. This is Morning Christina, Morning Christina, Morning Christina. How do you read me?

VTS: Morning Christina, this is Keelung VTS. I read you poor. ADVICE: Change to VHF Channel four two.

Morning Christina: Changing to VHF Channel four two. Do you copy?

VTS: Yes, I read you excellent.

Morning Christina: I'd like to inform you that I'm going to enter your VTS area.

VTS: Could you spell the name of your vessel, please?

Morning Cristina: My vessel's name is Morning Christina, Mike Oscar Romeo November India November Golf Charlie Hotel Romeo India Sierra Tango India November Alfa, over.

VTS: Roger. And your call sign and IMO number, sir?

Morning Christina: The call sign of my vessel is 3FKX8, and my IMO number is 9574054, over.

VTS:	What is your flag state?
Morning Christina:	My flag State is Panama, over
VTS:	Copy that, Morning Christina, your present course and speed?
Morning Christina:	My present course is 200 degree and my speed is 10 knots-mistake. Correction, my present speed is 8, zero-eight, knots, over.
VTS:	Thank you, Sir. From what direction are you approaching and the ETA in the entrance position?
Morning Christina:	I'm approaching the VTS area from the northbound and my ETA is 1600 local time, over.
VTS:	Understood. INFORMATION: MV Lalu is altering course to starboard. She will turn ahead of you. WARNING: Do not overtake the vessel ahead of you.
Morning Christina:	I will not overtake the vessel ahead of me, over.
VTS:	Morning Christina. Your present drafts, forward and aft as well as the maneuvering speed?
Morning Christina:	My draft forward is 10 meters and draft aft is 11 meters. My maneuvering speed is 8 knots, over.
VTS:	Morning Christina. Do you have any lists?
Morning Christina:	No, I have no list.
VTS:	Do you carry any dangerous goods?
Morning Christina:	No, I do not carry any dangerous goods, over.
VTS:	Roger, thank you, Sir. Stand by on VHF Channel four two.
Morning Christina:	Standing by on VHF Channel four two.
(after a while)	
Morning Christina:	Keelung VTS Station, Keelung VTS Station. This is Morning Christina. Do you copy?
VTS:	Morning Christina, please go ahead.

Morning Christina: QUESTION: Do I have permission to enter the main fairway?

VTS: ANSWER: You have permission to enter the main fairway.

Morning Christina: OK. Thank you very much.

Comprehension Questions : 🎧 Track 72

1. What advice does Keelung VTS Station give?
2. What vessel information does Keelung VTS Station ask?
3. What warning does Keelung VTS Station give?
4. How does Morning Christina respond to the warning?

Part Two: Grammar, Language and Cultural Tips

A. An Example of Helm Order 🎧 Track 73

Scenario: The MV Lalu is now ready to cast off and swing away from the berth.

Pilot:	Single up spring forward!
Captain:	Lalu Forward station, this is Lalu Bridge. Single up spring forward!
Forward station:	Lalu Bridge, this is Lalu Forward station. I will single up.
Captain:	Lalu Aft station, this is Lalu Bridge. Single up Aft breast line!
Aft station:	Lalu Bridge, this is Lalu Aft station. I will single up.
Forward station:	Lalu Bridge, singled up forward.
Aft station:	Lalu Bridge, singled up aft.
Pilot:	Let go forward! Let go aft!
Captain:	Lalu Forward station, this is Lalu Bridge. Let go forward!
Forward station:	Lalu Bridge, Let go, Sir.
Captain:	Lalu Aft station, this is Lalu Bridge. Let go aft!
Aft station:	Lalu Bridge, this is Lalu Aft station. Let go, Sir.

Forward station:	Lalu Bridge, all clear forward!
Aft station:	Lalu Bridge, all clear aft.
Pilot:	Wheel amidships, slow ahead.
The helmsman:	Wheel amidships. Slow ahead.
Pilot:	Starboard twenty!
The helmsman:	Starboard twenty!

B. Message Markers used by the VTS

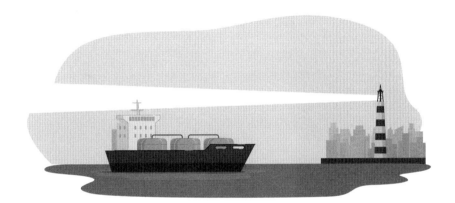

Vessel Traffic Services are provided as an air traffic controller for ships to make sure the ships come in and out a port safely. Every ship will report her arrival or departure to VTS before entering or leaving a port. VTS teams keep watch 24/7. They notify ships over the VHF of the essential and timely navigational information like reporting lines, traffic lane, separation zone and pilot boarding times to ensure the safety and efficiency of navigation in the water area. They also respond to the assistance that ships require. In order to avoid confusion in VTS communication, the following message markers are spoken preceding messages: information, advise, instruction, warning, question, answer, intention and request (from SMCP 2.4, IMO).

Message Markers	Implications
INFORMATION	This marker is preferably used for navigational and traffic information.
WARNING	This marker implies the intention of the sender to inform others about danger.
ADVICE	This marker implies the intention of the sender to influence others by a recommendation.
INSTRUCTION	This marker indicates the intention of the sender with full authority to influence others by a regulation.
QUESTION	This indicates that the recipient is expected to return an answer to the questions.
REQUEST	This indicates that the following message is asking for action.
ANSWER	This indicates that the following message is the reply to a previous question.
INTENTION	This indicates that the following message informs the immediate navigational action intended to be taken.

C. Ways of Using Modal Auxiliaries in SMCP

Use/expression	Auxiliaries	Examples
ability	can	Can you proceed? I can proceed without assistance
permission	do	Do I have permission to enter the main fairway? (X) May/Can I enter the main fairway?
advice		Do not overtake the vessel ahead of you.
receiving suggestion/inquiry	will	I will not overtake the vessel ahead of me. I will send pumps.
intention		I will abandon the vessel.
necessity	must	Must I take tugs?
expectation	should	The Master should give clear instructions.

Example:

The MV Lalu: Port service this is MV Lalu. How do you read me over?

Port service: This is port service I read good, go ahead over

The MV Lalu: Port service, we passed Beta Island on starboard side distance 1.5 miles over.

Port service:	MV Lalu, what is your present course and speed over?
The MV Lalu:	Port service, my present course is three zero zero degrees and speed one zero knots over. QUESTION. What is my anchor position over?
Port service:	your anchor position is one zero five degrees three miles from the lighthouse over.
The MV Lalu:	Port service. my anchor position is one zero five degrees three miles from the lighthouse. Is that correct over?
Port service:	That's correct you must anchor clear of the fairway over.
The MV Lalu:	Port service, I'll anchor clear of the ferry over.
Port service:	MV Lalu, you must call when you drop anchor a pilot station over.
The MV Lalu:	Port service I will call when I drop anchor at pilot station on channel one two over.
Port service:	MV Lalu, standby channel 12 out.

D. Articles with Geographical Names

"the" is used:

Oceans/Seas	The Pacific Ocean, The Arctic Sea, etc.
Areas	The Arctic, The Antarctic, the North of Los Angeles, etc.
Groups of Land	the Philippines
Channels/Straits/Rivers/canals	The English Channel, The Bashi Channel, The Nile, The Panama Canal, etc.
Mountains/Ranges of Mountains	the Himalayas, the Alps, etc.
Gulf	The Persian Gulf, The Gulf of Mexico, etc.
Countries	The Netherlands, the USA (abbreviation), the UK (abbreviation)

"the" is not used:

Continents	Asia, Europe, Africa, South America, etc.
Countries	Japan, Korea, France, Egypt, Turkey, etc.
Islands	Hawaii, Honshu Island, Hokkaido, etc.
Cities	New York, London, Calcutta, Melbourne, etc.

Part Three: Reading

Finding the location of Hong Kong in the latitude and longitude

Nautical charts pinpoint a specific place on Earth using lines of latitude and longitude. These lines are parallel and have an equal distance from each other. Latitude lines run horizontally indicating a place measured north or south of the equator. Therefore, the equator, the line going around the Earth and dividing it into the northern and southern hemispheres, is given a latitude of zero degree (0°). Values of degrees latitude are numbered from 0 to 90 north and south. In another word, the North Pole is 90 degree north, and the South Pole is 90 degrees south. While similar to latitude lines, longitude lines (also known as meridians) run vertically from east to west. Zero degrees longitude is located at Greenwich, England (known as Prime). The degrees increase 180 east and 180 west and finally meet at the International Date Line in the Pacific Ocean.

Latitude and longitude are measured in degrees, minutes, and seconds for precision purposes. Each degree is divided into 60 minutes, and there are 60 seconds in each minute. If we divide the Earth's surface by 360 degrees, the distance for each one degree of latitude or longitude is over 69 miles. But the Earth is in fact slightly egg-shaped. At 45 degrees N or S of the equator, one degree of longitude is about 49 miles. Navigators in shipping and aviation industries use nautical miles. One nautical mile represents one minute of latitude. Take Hong Kong as an example, it is marked as 22°15'0"N and 114°10'0"E. That means it is located at 22 degrees, 15 minutes, and 0 seconds north of the equator and 114 degrees, 10 minutes, and 0 seconds west of Greenwich, England. At sea, speed is measured in knots. One knot equals to one nautical mile per hour (about 1.852 kilometers). If the distance between two points on map is 240 nautical miles and the vessel's speed is 20 knots, it will take 12 hours from one point to another.

＊Read aloud the latitude and longitude of the following seaports:

Seaport	the latitude and longitude
Los Angeles, California	34°3'8" N/ 118°14'34"W
Sydney	40°17'3"N/ 84°9'20"W
Singapore	01°22'0"N/ 103°48'0"E
Shanghai	31°0'18"N/ 121°24'31"E

＊The distance from Tokyo to Los Angeles is 8772km. Figure out the distance between Tokyo and Los Angles in nautical miles.

＊The vessel is leaving Cape Town her way to Port Klang, Malaysia at 00:00 UTC, January 1. Her maximum speed is 17 knots. Use the following information to calculate the approximate arrival date.

The distance from Cape Town to Port Klang: 5152.4 nautical miles.

Part Four: More Exercises

A. Listen and write down the sentence. ⌒ Track 74

1. _____
2. _____
3. _____
4. _____
5. _____

B. Listen and Write. Listen to information about a harbor. Write down the information of a harbor based on what you hear. 🎧 **Track 75**

    1. the location of the port:

    2. the numbers of container berths:

C. Listen and Circle. Listen to a mariner's voyage and circle the correct answer. 🎧 **Track 76**

    1. The port of departure was Bombay/Dubai/Jakarta.

    2. The vessel was a passenger ship/oil tanker/bulker.

    3. The cyclone was in the Pacific Ocean/Indian Ocean.

    4. Jakarta/Manila was the last port of call.

    5. The mariner planned to visit a friend/get some supplies in Manila.

D. Find the locations of the following cities' latitudes and longitudes through the Internet.

    1. Taipei

    2. Cairo

    3. New York

    4. Montreal

    5. Mecca

國家圖書館出版品預行編目資料

IMO初級航海英語會話／王鳳敏作. -- 初版.
-- 臺北市：五南圖書出版股份有限公司,
2022.03
面； 公分
ISBN 978-626-317-575-4（平裝）

1.CST:英語 2.CST:航海 3.CST:會話

805.188   111000806

5I58

IMO初級航海英語會話

作　　者 ― 王鳳敏（8.4）

發 行 人 ― 楊榮川

總 經 理 ― 楊士清

總 編 輯 ― 楊秀麗

副總編輯 ― 王正華

責任編輯 ― 張維文

封面設計 ― 鄭云淨

出 版 者 ― 五南圖書出版股份有限公司

地　　址：106台北市大安區和平東路二段339號4樓

電　　話：(02)2705-5066　　傳　　真：(02)2706-6100

網　　址：https://www.wunan.com.tw

電子郵件：wunan@wunan.com.tw

劃撥帳號：01068953

戶　　名：五南圖書出版股份有限公司

法律顧問　林勝安律師事務所　林勝安律師

出版日期　2022年3月初版一刷

定　　價　新臺幣280元

經典永恆・名著常在

五十週年的獻禮 —— 經典名著文庫

五南，五十年了，半個世紀，人生旅程的一大半，走過來了。

思索著，邁向百年的未來歷程，能為知識界、文化學術界作些什麼？

在速食文化的生態下，有什麼值得讓人雋永品味的？

歷代經典・當今名著，經過時間的洗禮，千錘百鍊，流傳至今，光芒耀人；

不僅使我們能領悟前人的智慧，同時也增深加廣我們思考的深度與視野。

我們決心投入巨資，有計畫的系統梳選，成立「經典名著文庫」，

希望收入古今中外思想性的、充滿睿智與獨見的經典、名著。

這是一項理想性的、永續性的巨大出版工程。

不在意讀者的眾寡，只考慮它的學術價值，力求完整展現先哲思想的軌跡；

為知識界開啟一片智慧之窗，營造一座百花綻放的世界文明公園，

任君遨遊、取菁吸蜜、嘉惠學子！